SHADOW BRINGER

David Calcutt

OXFORD
UNIVERSITY PRESS

OXFORD
UNIVERSITY PRESS

Great Clarendon Street, Oxford OX2 6DP

Oxford University Press is a department of the University of Oxford.
It furthers the University's objective of excellence in research, scholarship,
and education by publishing worldwide in

Oxford   New York

Auckland   Cape Town   Dar es Salaam   Hong Kong   Karachi
Kuala Lumpur   Madrid   Melbourne   Mexico City   Nairobi
New Delhi   Shanghai   Taipei   Toronto

With offices in

Argentina   Austria   Brazil   Chile   Czech Republic   France   Greece
Guatemala   Hungary   Italy   Japan   Poland   Portugal   Singapore
South Korea   Switzerland   Thailand   Turkey   Ukraine   Vietnam

Oxford is a registered trade mark of Oxford University Press
in the UK and in certain other countries

British Library Cataloguing in Publication Data

Data available

ISBN: 978-0-19-272926-2

1 3 5 7 9 10 8 6 4 2

Printed in Great Britain by CPI Cox and Wyman, Reading, Berkshire

Paper used in the production of this book is a natural,
recyclable product made from wood grown in sustainable forests.
The manufacturing process conforms to the environmental
regulations of the country of origin.

Praise for *Shadow Bringer*

'a remarkable novel, gripping, written with care . . .
It's a rare treat to find a novel written by an author
who has plainly listened hard to every word he
writes'   *Carousel*

'A haunting and powerful psychological thriller . . .
With beautifully drawn characters and a real sense of
brooding menace, the author has succeeded in
blending reality with magic to create a novel that is
incredibly tense and atmospheric.'
                                                        Lovereading4kids.co.uk

'a strong, bold and perceptive book that is both
insightful and enjoyable'   *School Librarian*

'a spooky and entertaining read'   *Writeaway*

'I really enjoyed this and would recommend it to
anyone who enjoys a few shivers down their spine.'
                                            Marie-Louise Jensen, author

'*Shadow Bringer* is a lovely, lovely book. Part
psychological thriller, part supernatural dream, part
coming-of-age story, I'd recommend it to any
thoughtful reader . . . Their parents will love it too.'
                                                        thebookbag.co.uk

Other books by David Calcutt

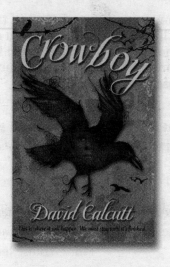

Contents

To my wife, Sue, and my children, Matt, Jon and Helen

One

The Creature

It slept.

It lay at the bottom of all things.

Without shape, without form, without height, without depth. Growing, shrinking, rising, falling. Ebb and flow, tremble and pulse.

A creature of darkness dwelling in darkness.

Not breathing.

But sleeping, and dreaming.

Chaos and confusion, turmoil, upheaval. Things splitting, things falling apart. It dreamed worlds collapsing, suns exploding. Unmaking and unravelling, the flux of destruction. It dreamed fire, flood, warfare, ruin.

These were what it fed on. From these it took its strength and power. These dreams were what it was for.

Sometimes a call came. A name spoken, a challenge made. Then it let its power stir. It roused itself and rose from the darkness, it found its form and made itself known. Then, as monster, or giant, or ogre, or demon, it strode across the earth and waged war. To taste the thrill of battle and blood-shed, to fight and to kill beneath the fierce sun.

Sometimes it was victor. Sometimes vanquished. It didn't matter.

What mattered was the contest, the joy of destruction.

Things splitting, things falling apart.

And now, again, a call came. Little more than a whisper, from far off, a voice. Falling, spinning, a flickering spark, a flash of light in the darkness. A shining hook dropped in the black pool. A name spoken. The creature felt the voice pierce the depth of its being. It heard the name spoken. It stirred. It woke.

There was a burst of light, a rush of air.

The creature drew breath and spoke.

I'm coming to get you.

Two

Something Was Watching

Something was watching him.

He stood by the hedge looking over into the field. It was bare and churned into brown furrows, lumps of earth and stones, stretching away uphill towards the main road. He could hear traffic in the distance. There were birds in the field pecking over the ground. Crows and starlings and woodpigeons. The sky above the field was grey. It had rained a few days before and the earth was muddy. It gave him a hollow feeling.

And the feeling of being watched.

Something out there. Hidden among the furrows and the birds. Invisible behind the pale, damp light.

Something without a shape, that he couldn't put a name to.

He'd had a dream the night before. The first night he'd stayed at his aunt and uncle's. After his mother had gone away on holiday. In the dream he'd heard his mother's voice calling to him, his name, over and over, from far off. Then her voice had suddenly come close, as if speaking into his ear, and it was no longer his mother's voice, it was another's, deeper and harsher. He'd woken suddenly, breathing fast and hard.

Now the dream came back to him. The deep, harsh voice. And something out there watching him.

He bent down and picked up a stone from the towpath. It was heavy in his hand, rough edged, gritty, and solid. He threw the stone as hard and as far as he could into the field to chase the thing away. Even before it hit the ground, the birds that were feeding there sprang up in a racket and panic of flight. Clap and tumble of woodpigeons, wheel and screech and scatter of starlings. The slow, rag-winged flap of the crows, raking and scratching the air with their voices. The birds wheeled away across the sky, and were gone. The field was empty. And it was looking at him.

Something touched his leg.

He turned. The dog was standing beside him. He reached down and ruffled her neck and she nuzzled against his hand. She was his uncle's dog, a black and white collie, and his uncle had said he could take her for a walk along the canal, as long as he didn't take her lead off until they were well away from the road. He unclipped the lead from her collar now and looped it around his waist.

'Stay,' he said, and held his hand above her head as his uncle had shown him. The dog sat, ears erect, eyes alert, her tail brushing backwards and forwards across the gravel and mud of the towpath. He stroked her neck again.

'Fields don't look at people, do they, Whistle?' he said to her. He straightened himself and glanced back across the field.

Nothing there.

He turned back to the dog.

'Come on, Whistle,' he said. 'Let's go!'

He set off running as fast as he could along the towpath, and Whistle gave a yelp and went bounding along beside him, and then ahead of him, and he kept on running, calling out, 'Let's go, let's go, let's go!' until he couldn't call out any more and was out of breath and had to stop.

He'd thought running would get rid of the feeling, but it hadn't. It was still there.

He turned round, quickly. Nothing there. The hedge, the fields. The empty sky. And something watching.

No.

'Stupid,' he said, and turned back.

There was a track leading off the towpath to the left that led up and round on to an old hump-backed bridge over the canal. He took the track and climbed onto the bridge and stood looking back the way he'd come. The dog followed him and snuffled among the tufts of grass and weeds that grew from the crumbling brickwork.

He leaned against the bridge, following the curve of the canal with his eyes. The field to the right was full of birds again, and away beyond the field he could see the high-rise flats that stood near the centre of town. He was far away from there now, far from where he lived with his mother, staying with an aunt and uncle he hardly knew. He felt that loneliness again that he'd felt the night before, lying awake in the dark in a strange room before he slept and the dream came, and shut his eyes against it. He tried to lose himself in the cawing of the crows in the field, and the distant drone of the traffic on the motorway, but it was no good. He squeezed his eyes shut tighter, trying to block everything out. Then the voice that had spoken in his dream spoke to him again.

Close. Deep and harsh.

He opened his eyes and looked round sharply to his right.

Something there?

The path from the bridge led down into the ploughed field and over to the right at the corner of the field there was a wood. And he was looking at the sky above the wood. The grey, empty sky. And something was looking at him out of the emptiness.

He shivered. And then the dog began to growl.

He looked down. She was standing beside him with her ears and tail up and her head thrust forward, looking down towards the wood, and making a low growling deep in her throat.

'What is it, girl?' he said to her. 'What's the matter?'

He petted her but he could feel how her body was tensed under his hand, and that she was quivering all over. He took his hand away and looked up again and then he saw it.

First there had been nothing, just the pale light, the high cloud. Then there was something, as if the sky had blinked and this thing had appeared.

Something black and shapeless floating in the sky.

He told himself it must be a crow, but he knew it wasn't. It was too big for a crow, and crows didn't move like this thing was moving. It wasn't flying. It was floating. So perhaps it was a bin-liner, blown up there by the wind. But there was no wind.

Everything was still.

A stretched-tight stillness, waiting for something to happen.

He watched the thing in the air, the way it moved, turning and twisting round and back on itself. Writhing, struggling as if trying to find a shape for itself.

It didn't seem to have any shape at all.

And now Nathan realized that he was scared. His stomach was tight and his throat was dry. He was gripped by the terror of that twisting shapeless thing in the sky.

It was time to go. Get away from here, run all the way back down the towpath to the other bridge and then up onto the road and back to his uncle's house. Forget about this thing. Think about what it might have been later, when he was safe.

He didn't feel safe now.

But before he could go the thing suddenly flipped over and seemed to fold in on itself and dropped down below the trees into the wood.

And the dog gave a yelp and went racing off the bridge down the track into the field.

Nathan called after her but she didn't stop. She kept running and he could see her making her way down to the edge of the field and then turning and heading towards the trees. In a few minutes she'd be there. So he set off running as well, calling her name over and over as he ran, his feet crunching against the wet gravel of the track.

As he came closer to the trees he saw that Whistle had stopped at the edge of the wood, so he stopped too, to catch his breath. Her body was tensed and her ears were erect and she was staring into the trees. As if she could see something in there. From where he stood he called out to her.

'Whistle! Whistle! Come, girl! Come!'

She didn't move, so he tried again.

'Come, Whistle! Bone! Come and have a bone.'

His uncle had told him that, whatever Whistle was doing, the word 'bone' usually made her leave it and come running. And he thought that's what she was going to do, because she turned and looked back at him, and he called out, 'Good girl, Whistle! Come! Bone! Come on!'

But she didn't come. She turned back and trotted in among the trees.

'Bloody dog,' he said aloud.

He stood for a few moments on the track looking at the wood. The topmost branches of the trees were brittle against the sky. They didn't have their leaves yet. Beneath them all was darkness and tangles of shadow. Scattered thoughts flicked through his brain. Crows in the field. Ragged wings, voices scratching. His name spoken in the dark.

Something watching.

'Just a bin-liner,' he said.

Then he went on along the track towards the wood.

Three

The Lime Pits

As soon as he entered the wood he was in semi-darkness. The trees grew so closely together that even on a bright day they let in only a little light. And today was not a bright day. It was quiet too. Outside the wood, in the fields or by the canal, there was always the low and steady hum of traffic in the background from the motorway and from the town. But in here that noise was shut off. The wood kept it out. It had its own sounds. Birdsong. Wing clap. Leaf rustle. Twig snap. Stream water rattling over stones.

Where the wood grew now used to be an open pit where limestone had been dug. But then, about a hundred years ago, the pit had been filled with water and trees planted around it. Now it was as if the wood and the pool that lay at the centre of it had always been there. The only clue was in the name given to the wood and its surrounding area. The Lime Pits. The farm nearby, to which all the land belonged, was called Limepits Farm.

He followed a path that ran along high above a stream and led to a wooden bridge with high metal rails on either side. The pool lay to the left of the bridge and the stream ran under the bridge into the pool. He stopped there and leaned on the rail, looking out over the water. He knew that the path ran all the way around the pool because he'd come here a year or so ago with his father, the two of them riding their bikes all the way along the canal to reach it. It had been one of the last days he'd been out with his father and he remembered everything about it, and everything his father had told him about the Lime Pits and their history.

Out in the middle of the pool there was a small island. Beyond that the pool narrowed and curved to the right to disappear among high, steep banks thickly grown with trees. Many of their branches hung out low over the water. Nearer the island, another tree leaned out from its bank with its branches too hanging over the water. One of these branches had a long rope tied to it, and it looked as if someone had put it there so that they could swing out over to the island. He couldn't remember if the rope had been there when he'd been here with his father.

He stood gazing at the rope, the pool, the island. The dark water beyond, the tree shadows. He heard the silence. He felt the stillness.

There was no sign of the dog.

He knew he ought to call her. If he called her she'd probably come running. Then he'd put the lead on her and they'd go back. He should call her. But he didn't call her. He didn't want to call out into that silence. He didn't want his voice falling into that stillness.

There might be something else that would hear him.

He looked up to where the sky showed through the gap in the treetops above the pool. It would have come down through there.

What would have?

That.

What had come down?

That thing.

What thing? What was it?

He saw it again, twisting in the sky above the trees. Then he saw it fold and drop. He watched it come down through the gap in the trees, saw it floating gliding winding coiling down to touch the water, and rest on the surface of the water, and then—

And then what?

To sink.

To float glide wind coil down through the water and come to rest on the bottom.

There now, down at the bottom. In the cold dark.

Still watching him. And waiting. For what?

Where was the dog?

Suddenly there came a sharp rasp of sound, and a movement, and something leapt out from under the bridge and lifted up into the air. He gave a cry and staggered back, flinging his arm up to protect himself, and the thing cried out as well, that harsh and rasping ratchet of voice, and he glimpsed a grey form unfolding, a long neck snaking forwards, and heard the slap and thump of wings beating the air.

It was a heron, disturbed from its resting place by his presence on the bridge. Now it was flying with slow wingbeats low across the water towards the island and then swerving over and following the curve of the pool round, to find a place where it could rest undisturbed, in the thicker and darker part of the wood. Nathan watched it. His heart was still beating fast from the fright the bird had given him.

But the heron breaking out like that had made the woods and the pool seem ordinary again. He could hear other sounds now, the twitters and pipings of small birds among the branches, he saw their movements, their hoppings and scurryings and quick bursts of flight. There were ripples on the water. Pale light glittered.

He thought he'd better go and find Whistle.

But just then there came a loud 'kraaark!' from across the pool, and the heron reappeared, swinging back across the water, lifting up, and flying over the tops of the trees and away. He heard its cry again from beyond the wood, 'kraaark! kraaark!'

Something had alarmed it. Something over there on the other side of the pool. Among the trees. Or in the water.

Lying at the bottom. In the cold dark.

He heard Whistle barking.

From across the pool. The same place.

That's what had disturbed the heron. Whistle.

He ran off the bridge and along the path, then veered to the left up some steps that led to the high bank and round to the other side of the pool. And all the time he was running Whistle kept up her barking, and he tried not to think about what she might be barking at, and that maybe it hadn't been her after all that had disturbed the heron, and that maybe what had disturbed the heron was the same thing that Whistle was barking at now. He tried not to think about any of that, he tried to empty his head and think only of what he was doing right now, which was running, one foot going in front of another, dodging the brambles that grew out over the track, jumping over a fallen tree trunk, taking more steps up, through the rotted and half-tumbled remains of a gate and onto the highest part of the bank, the darkest part of the wood, the other side of the pool.

He was there.

But Whistle wasn't. And she had stopped barking.

He looked around but he couldn't see her. He called her name and his voice echoed in the stillness of the place and there was no answering yelp or whine.

Then a voice spoke.

It wanted you to come here.

The words were so clear in his head that he thought for a moment they'd been spoken out loud. But he knew there was no one out there to speak them.

He heard the voice again.

It's waiting for you.

And he knew then that it had been spoken not out loud but in his head. He also knew that it was not his voice.

It was like the voice that had spoken in his bad dream.

He leaned his back against a tree and gripped the trunk with his fingers to stop himself from running away. There's nothing here, he told himself. You just remembered that voice from your dream. Nothing called you. Nothing wanted you to come here. He spoke aloud.

16

'It was just a bin-liner.'

He let go of the trunk and stood up straight. He was all right. This was just the Lime Pits. Whistle was here somewhere. Now he was going to find her and put the lead on her collar and take her back home.

He walked slowly along the track that led around the pool. It was long and narrow and deep here and the trees grew closely together along the top of the bank so that little light came through from above. Some of the trees leaned out over the pool almost at right angles. There was a closed-in feel about the place, a gloomy stillness that made you walk through it quietly, listening. Sometimes it was as if the place was listening to you.

The time he'd come here with his father, they'd been walking together along the track when his father had stopped suddenly and had pointed down at the pool and told him to look. He had peered over the edge and seen what he had thought at first was a broken-off piece of branch floating just beneath the surface of the water. But then a patch of sunlight had dappled across the surface of the pool and he had seen a flash of deep gold and a slow stirring of fins and a long, hooked jaw.

'That's a pike,' his father had said to him. 'It's a real killer. A monster.'

He had never seen the pike again, nor any other fish down there. But whenever he came to this end of the pool he remembered it, and the word 'monster' came into his head.

He was looking down at the dark water now. The bank was steep and high and in places its sides dropped almost straight down where earth and clay had crumbled and fallen into the pool. Roots of trees stuck out from the sides of the bank. One of them looked like a huge, thick-bodied snake twisting out of its hole and sliding down into the water. How far down did it go? To the bottom? He tried to follow it all the way down through the dark water to the bottom of the pool. He imagined the tip of the root down there buried in the black mud.

There was a scuffle of movement along the bank from where the root went into the water. In the undergrowth down by the waterline. He turned to look and saw the dog.

She was crouched on a narrow ledge that stuck out a few feet into the pool and was scrabbling at the bank with her front paws, trying to climb up. But the bank was too steep and too overgrown. He didn't think about how she'd come to be down there. Nathan ran along the track to where she was and knelt down and leaned over the edge and called to her.

'Whistle! Come on! Up you come!'

She looked up and saw him and barked and scrabbled furiously at the bank and tried to pull herself up. She managed a little way but then got stuck and dropped back. He called to her again and this time she didn't try to climb up but stood at the bottom on the ledge looking up at him. Her tail was wagging and he could hear her whining.

Yes, OK, I'll come down and get you. Easy.

A little way along the track was a place where the bank wasn't so steep, and there were roots sticking out that he could hold on to. Climbing back up with the dog would be more of a problem, but he didn't think too much about that. One thing at a time. Get down first.

It wasn't that difficult. He kept his body turned to the side, and lowered himself from root to root, pushing into the earth with his feet to stop his body from pitching forward and over. Within a few minutes he was at the bottom and Whistle was beside him, whimpering and rubbing her nose and head against his legs. He unlooped the lead from around his waist and fastened the clasp to her collar.

'OK,' he said aloud. 'Now we're both down here. So how do we get back up? Any ideas?'

The dog looked at him and looked up the bank and wagged her tail.

'What did you come down here for anyway?'

19

He was standing close to the water on the ledge. Where it entered the water the ledge didn't slope in smoothly. It dropped straight down. He followed the drop with his eyes but he couldn't see to the bottom.

And something was down there, deep under the water. Dropped down out of the sky. Black and shapeless. Lying there at the bottom.

He took a step so that he stood right on the edge, the water touching the tips of his shoes. He heard Whistle growling and whimpering behind him.

'It's OK, girl,' he said. 'We'll go back up in a bit.'

But as he spoke he was staring at the water, down into the darkness of the pool, and it seemed to him that there was another darkness there; not the pool's darkness, but the darkness of something else. Something that lay inside the pool but was separate from it. Darker than the pool's darkness. And that darkness was all he saw. It was all he was aware of. Rising up from the bottom of the pool, rising towards him.

A real killer. A monster.

Something grabbed his foot.

He gasped. Bony fingers gripped his ankle, squeezing tight. He felt a coldness running up his leg, felt that grip pulling at him, dragging him down, into the water. He jerked his foot away sharply and fell back against the bank.

His right trainer and the lower part of his jeans were soaking wet. His right foot inside the trainer was wet as well. The trainer was filled with the water. He could feel his foot squelching inside it. He had stepped into the water. He must have done. Without knowing it he'd lowered his right foot down into the pool. As if he'd been going to jump in. He'd done that, and he hadn't known he'd done it.

But something had known. Something had been watching him. Calling him. Waiting for him. And when he'd done it, it had reached up and grabbed hold of him.

The thing down there. The thing that had fallen out of the sky.

He stood up. The dog was standing beside him with the lead attached to her collar and the other end lying on the ground. At some point he must have loosed it. He didn't remember doing that either. He picked up the lead and put his hand through the loop and lashed it twice around his fingers to make sure he had a good grip. Then he spoke to the dog, making his voice as loud and ordinary as he could.

'Good dog,' he said. 'Come on. We're going now.'

With the lead wrapped around his left hand he reached up with his right and grabbed hold of a root and began to pull himself up. And now that she had the security of the lead Whistle was able to take firmer hold and climb without falling back. So between them, sometimes the boy pulling the dog, and sometimes the dog pulling the boy, they managed to clamber and crawl and scrabble their way back to the top.

He sat on the bank keeping the lead lashed around his wrist and took off his trainer. He turned it over and dark scummy water ran out onto the earth. Then he put it back on again and fastened it and stood up. His foot still squelched inside, and the right leg of his jeans was soaking wet. He was hot with the effort of the climb and he unzipped his jacket. The jacket, and the jumper underneath, were filthy and stained with mud and moss. So were his jeans. His hands and face were dirty too. He smelt of stagnant water. He'd be in for it when he got back. But he wanted to get back all the same.

'Let's go,' he said to the dog.

But he didn't move. He stayed where he was. He looked across towards the middle of the pool where the island was. The heron had returned and was standing among the reeds that grew around the side of the island. Its head was drawn into its neck. Alert, watching, hunting.

He lifted his gaze to the patch of sky above the island. He thought of the black thing floating down through the trees towards the pool. He saw it falling again, followed it down, and his gaze came to rest on the surface of the pool.

He followed it down through the dark water.

Nothing, he said to himself. There couldn't be. Things like that.

Things like what.

Cold fingers gripping his foot.

A scratching in the air.

A voice in his head. A voice out there.

It wanted you to come. It called you.

He was looking down into the dark water.

There was a darkness in his head.

The darkness and the dark water were looking at him.

Four

Smoke Vision

She is gazing as if through dark water.

The girl sits in the hut of woven branches and beside her sits the Old Woman. Smoke from a small fire burning in front of her drifts upwards in slow swirls and the smell from the smoke is strong and sweet and the girl inhales it deeply. The Old Woman lifts her hand and passes it back and forth across the girl's face, but the girl does not blink. Her eyes are wide and unmoving and they stare through the smoke at the vision it shapes.

Dark water, and twists of weed, shivers of movement, undulations of shadow. And far off a wrinkle of light.

The Old Woman sees the girl's body grow tense. Her spine stiffens, her lips draw back from her teeth, her palms press into the earth, her fingers make claws. The Old Woman speaks softly, perhaps to herself, perhaps to others unseen who are also present.

'She is seeing it.'

She is seeing the creature that lies beneath the water, settled in the ooze and mud of the bottom, and how sometimes it seems to be one with that ooze and mud, and how at others it separates from them with slow wave-like movements, that are heavy too, with a drag and pull as if tugging at roots buried deep within its own centre. And now she is feeling that drag and weight herself, and the bright stab of pain that twists inside her like a hook, and stabs and twists and stabs again, and the creature jolts and shudders, and she jolts and shudders, as it wrenches itself into being.

Low in her throat, the Old Woman begins to sing the song of calling back.

The girl hears the song but it is distant and she is one with the creature now and letting its strength grow within and through her. She knows the danger in this and is ready to reach out and grasp the thread of the Old Woman's song that is flinging itself slowly towards her. So she will wind the song about her and be lifted back to the safety of the hut. But even as she takes hold of it she looks up and sees far off in the splintered sunlight above a human face.

She gasps, and the song catches in the Old Woman's throat, who gives a gasp herself, and reaches out her hands as if to take hold of the girl, as if the girl is in danger of falling into some deep chasm and being lost for ever. But at that same moment the girl blinks and turns her head and her eyes are looking not into the smoke-vision but at the Old Woman.

'Rasha?'

'Give me some water.'

The Old Woman takes the stone bowl in which the fire is burning and moves it aside. Then she picks up a bowl of wood and gives it to the girl. The girl takes it and puts it to her lips and drinks, then lowers the bowl to her lap.

'The creature is there,' she says. 'In the other world. It is beginning to make its shape.'

She lifts the bowl and drinks from it again, and hands the bowl back to the Old Woman. Their fingers touch as the bowl passes from one to the other.

'This isn't all,' says the Old Woman.

The girl takes her hands from the bowl and the Old Woman places it back on the earth floor.

'There is another who has seen it,' says the girl. 'It has fixed on him. Already it is beginning to feed.' She pauses for a moment, then she says, 'Soon it will be time for hunting.'

'Soon,' says the Old Woman, 'but not yet.' She looks hard and unblinking into the girl's eyes. 'If you fail in your hunting you will not return.'

'I know,' says the girl.

'So you must have weapons,' says the Old Woman. 'Weapons that will not fail you. Weapons of power.'

The girl sees something in the Old Woman's eyes that makes her stomach tight with fear. It is like a fist clenched inside her, and her body stiffens about it. But her voice remains even when she speaks.

'Where will I find these weapons?'

The Old Woman holds her gaze.

'Not in this place,' she says.

What the girl can see in the Old Woman's eyes is a deep and impenetrable darkness, and something waiting beyond that darkness.

'I must take another journey,' she says.

'Yes,' says the Old Woman.

'Then let me take it,' says the girl. 'Tell me where I must go.'

The Old Woman lowers her head and shuts her eyes. Narrow bands of sunlight that filter through the woven branches of the hut fall across her bowed shoulders, the fur robe draped across them, the white hair that hangs loose across that robe. For some moments she is still, and the girl waits. Then she lifts her head and speaks softly as she stares once more into the girl's eyes.

'You must take your weapons from the cave of the Bear.'

The girl's eyelids flicker and she breathes in

sharply. But she says nothing and straightens her back and lays the palms of her hands flat on the floor. The Old Woman places the stone bowl with its glowing embers in front of her and feeds it with a handful of the dried and crushed leaves from the pouch that hangs about her neck. They crackle among the embers and small flames flicker upwards and she blows on the flames and the sweet smoke rises.

Rasha breathes in. She stares ahead.

From the floor beside her the Old Woman picks up a small one-sided drum. It has a wooden frame and a skin stretched tightly across the frame and fixed in place with knotted leather thongs. Around the edge of the frame are scratched and painted figures, some of animals, some of creatures part-animal, part-human. A bird with a woman's face. A man with the hooves and antlers of a stag. The Old Woman lays this drum across the girl's lap.

'Begin,' she says.

Rasha raises one hand above the drum. She continues to stare ahead. Then she brings her hand down and strikes.

Five

Frogspawn

When he got back the kitchen door was open but there was nobody in the house. Whistle ran into the kitchen ahead of him and took a drink from her water bowl then went on out of the kitchen into the living room. He looked out of the window and saw his grandad down at the bottom of the garden bent over the pond. He looked in the living room. Whistle was making a bed for herself on the settee with the cushions, and there was mud all over them. There was mud all over the carpet as well.

He went upstairs and took off his dirty clothes and stuffed them in the laundry basket, then washed himself in the bathroom, and went into his room and put some clean clothes on. He was trying not to think about what had happened. He didn't want to think about it. He'd think about it later.

If there was anything to think about. The memory of it was already growing hazy.

He sat down suddenly on the edge of the bed. He stared at the carpet. He was tired and a little shivery and there was a fuzziness in his head. A kind of faint humming or buzzing from far off. He shook his head to try and clear it.

After a few minutes he stood up and went downstairs. Whistle was still curled up on the settee. He took a dustpan and brush from the cupboard under the sink and tried to sweep the mud off the carpet. It didn't look much better. He put the dustpan and brush back then went outside to talk to his grandad.

His grandad was squatting beside the pond, fixing some green netting to its edge with large stones. He looked up and nodded.

'Hello, Nathan,' he said. 'Have a good walk?'

'Yes, thanks,' said Nathan, and he stood on the path beside the pond and watched as his grandad turned back to his work.

It was a large pond at the bottom of the garden in front of the fence. There was a rockery around it with plants growing in between the rocks and an apple tree nearby. His grandad had told him how he'd built the pond himself years ago just after he'd retired. He'd described to him how he'd dug out the hole and lined it with concrete, then lined the bottom with gravel and placed rocks of different sizes in, and filled it with water.

He'd put in plants to give the water oxygen and put in some water lilies too. He'd also built the rockery.

'But it was your grandmother who planted the apple tree,' he'd said. 'She grew it in a pot from a pip, and when it was big enough she planted it there, next to the pond. And look at it now. You'd think it had been there for ever. It gives some lovely apples in the autumn.'

He had never known his grandmother. She'd died before he was born. Whenever his grandad spoke about her a little croak came into his voice. He didn't talk about her much. What he liked talking about most was his pond and his rockery. He talked about it now as he placed the last stone on the netting.

'I put this on to keep the birds out,' he said. 'They'll eat the frogspawn if I don't.'

'There's frogspawn?' said Nathan.

'Yes,' said his grandad. 'A whole load of it there in the middle.'

Nathan looked but he couldn't see anything.

'That's because of the netting,' said his grandad. 'But it's there, all right. I spotted it yesterday so I went out and bought this netting.' He gazed down at the pond, then he said, 'I had something to tell you.'

'What?' said Nathan.

'It's about the computer.'

'What about the computer?'

'Something,' said his grandad. 'Theresa told me to tell you. It's gone. You'll have to wait until she comes back. My memory's getting worse.'

Theresa was his aunt's name. His uncle was named Rob. He asked his grandad where they were.

'At the supermarket,' he said. 'They do the week's shopping on Saturday mornings.'

'Oh,' said Nathan. He and his mum did their weekly shop on Thursday evenings. There were usually quite a few special offers then. And she sometimes had to work Saturday mornings. 'Has Kevin gone with them?' he said.

'I don't know where Kevin is,' said his grandad. 'I never do.' He raised his hand and called Nathan over to him. He was on the other side of the pond. 'Squat down over here,' he said. 'You'll be able to see the frogspawn.'

He walked round the side of the pond, stepping carefully over the rockery, and squatted next to his grandad. Last year he and his friend Joe had gone over to the pool and collected some frogspawn in jars and he'd taken the jar back home and left it on the windowsill and watched every day as the little black circles inside the jelly became more and more elongated and eventually hatched out as tadpoles. Then he'd taken the tadpoles in the jar back to the pool and emptied them into the water. But now he didn't want to think about frogspawn, and he didn't want to see it. He didn't look at the pond.

'What about when the tadpoles hatch out?' he asked his grandad.

'What about it?' said his grandad.

'When the tadpoles turn into frogs they won't be able to get out,' he said. 'Because of the netting.'

'I'll take it off when that happens,' said his grandad. Then his grandad told him a story about when some frogspawn had hatched a couple of years ago. A lot of the tadpoles had died but some had survived, and changed into frogs. Little green frogs, he said, no bigger than a fingernail. And he'd been down at the pond one morning and seen one of these little green frogs at the side of the pool, and suddenly a large spider had darted out from under a rock and grabbed the frog in its jaws and dragged it back under the stone.

'I didn't know spiders ate frogs,' said Nathan.

'Neither did I,' said his grandad. 'And I wouldn't have believed it if I hadn't seen it.'

Nathan thought of the little frog being dragged under the stone. He thought of the spider injecting it with poison so that it became paralysed, like they did with insects, and then sucking all the blood out of it.

And he thought of the cold fingers grabbing his foot and trying to drag him under the water of the pool. He was aware again of the buzzing in the back of his head, the fuzziness.

'It's horrible,' he said.

'It's nature,' said his grandad.

It felt as if it was time to go back in. He thought about trying to do something more about the muddy carpet and settee before his aunt and uncle came back from the supermarket, although he wasn't sure what. Suddenly he felt tired again and weak, and his knees began to tremble. But now his grandad was taking a stone off one of the corners of the netting.

'I'll lift the netting,' said his grandad. 'Then you can see the frogspawn better.'

He lifted the netting back and away from the surface of the pond. There was nothing Nathan could do about it now. He had to stay where he was and look. So he looked.

It was a large, shapeless, jellied mass of glistening black lying just under the surface of the water. Darker than the water. He knew how it felt when you plunged your hands into it and lifted it up, cold and slimy, green water and strings of loose jelly sliding out between your fingers. Twisting and turning. And the other thing, twisting and turning in the sky, dropping beneath the trees. Sinking through the dark water, lying at the bottom. Watching him. Waiting for him. Fingers reaching up, cold and slimy, gripping his leg, pulling him down.

The buzzing in his head grew louder. A black shadow began to gather there and the buzzing was coming out of the black shadow. His legs were trembling and there was a tingling in his fingers and the dark mass of the frogspawn began to pulse and throb. He put his hands on to the concrete sides of the pool to steady himself.

'Are you all right?' said his grandad.

'Yes,' he said. 'I'm fine.' His voice sounded thin and far off.

'You look like you've gone dizzy.'

'I'm OK, Grandad,' he said, and to prove it he pushed himself up from the pond and grinned. 'I think I'll go back in the house.'

'All right,' said his grandad, and he lowered the netting and secured it again with the stone.

He felt he ought to say something before he went, to show that everything was fine.

'Thanks for showing me the frogspawn.'

'We'll keep an eye on it every day,' said his grandad. 'Watch the tadpoles develop. And after you've gone back home perhaps you can come over at weekends and see them change into frogs.'

'I will,' said Nathan. 'And make sure the spiders don't get them.'

His grandad smiled and he smiled at his grandad and then he turned and walked back along the path across the middle of the lawn to the house, trying to keep his legs steady. All he wanted to do was get back to the house and go upstairs and lie down and wait for the tiredness to pass and the buzzing in his head to go away, but when he went into the kitchen his cousin Kevin was there.

He was sitting at the table in the middle of the kitchen eating a thick slab of sandwich and drinking Coke from a bottle. His cousin looked up when he came in.

'You stink,' he said.

'No, I don't,' said Nathan.

'You do,' said Kevin. 'You stink worse than the dog, and she stinks bad. What you been doing?'

His cousin was a year older than he was, taller and broader. There was something about him that made Nathan feel nervous, even though most of the time Kevin ignored him completely. Probably because Kevin didn't want him to be there, Nathan thought. But he wasn't ignoring him now.

'I just took Whistle along the canal,' said Nathan. 'And then over to the Lime Pits.'

'Over them or in them?' said Kevin.

'Whistle went down the bank and got stuck,' said Nathan. 'I had to climb down and get her back. I've had a wash and changed my clothes,' he added.

Kevin grinned.

'It didn't work,' he said. 'You stink. The dog stinks. And the settee stinks, and the carpet.' He took a big bite out of his sandwich and gulped down some Coke. 'Mum'll have something to say about it when she gets back.'

And he was right. She did. His aunt started almost as soon as she and Uncle Rob came back with the shopping, and she kept on all the time they were putting it away. The state of his clothes. The state of the dog. The state of the carpet. The state of the settee. She couldn't believe that Nathan had let the dog go into the living room, the state she was in, let alone get on the settee. Couldn't he see how filthy she was? Why hadn't he made her at least stay in the kitchen? And why hadn't he showered, or had a bath? Did he know what he smelled like? He'd not only got one set of clothes filthy and smelly but he'd made the clean clothes he'd put on smelly as well. Now he'd have to have a bath and change his clothes again, and the dog would have to have a bath, and the carpet would have to be cleaned, and the settee, and this was her only day off, she had a shift to do at the supermarket tomorrow, and now she'd have to spend the rest of it cleaning and washing.

That's how she was, his aunt Theresa. His mum had warned him about her before she left.

'She's a good woman,' his mum had said to him, 'and it's very kind of her to look after you while I'm away. But mind yourself while you're there. She's quite house-proud and likes things done her way.'

She certainly did.

Kevin was sitting at the table finishing his sandwich and grinning while all this was going on, and his uncle had been sent to get the dog showered, filthy animal, that was the least he could do for letting the boy take the dog off on his own all that way. And Kevin could do more than sit there stuffing his face as well, he could help her put the shopping away. And Kevin said something, he didn't hear what, it was getting difficult to catch all the words now, and there was his aunt's voice and there was Kevin's voice snapping at each other hard and sharp like the doors to the cupboards and the fridge and the freezer slammed hard and sharp as his aunt put the shopping away. And the snapping and the slamming was getting mixed up with the buzzing in his head that was growing louder all the time, and the buzzing was coming out of the black cloud that was forming there, a shapeless thing that swirled like smoke or black mist, and it didn't help that his face was flushed and tears were stinging his eyes and the tingling at the end of his fingers was beginning to spread into his hands and wrists.

The kitchen door opened and his grandad came in and started saying something to him. Something about the computer again. He heard the word 'e-mail' and tried to hear the rest of it, but then his aunt was talking.

'Didn't you tell him?'

'I couldn't remember.'

'I told you to tell him.'

'I'm telling him now.'

His grandad went to the sink and turned on the tap and held his hands under the running water. Then he turned off the tap and took a folded tea towel from the draining board.

'Don't use that,' said his aunt. 'It's for drying the dishes.'

'There isn't anything else to use,' said his grandad, and he wiped his hands dry on the tea towel and dropped it back unfolded on the draining board.

'What e-mail?' said Nathan. The buzzing had grown quieter and the black mist was fading a little but they were still there.

'You've got an e-mail,' said his grandad. 'On the computer.'

'I told him to tell you,' said his aunt. 'Before we went shopping.'

'I told him about the computer,' said his grandad. 'Didn't I?'

'But you forgot about the e-mail.'

'What e-mail,' said Nathan again. 'Who's it from?'

Their voices were still snapping.

'He does it on purpose,' said Kevin.

'That's enough of that,' said his aunt.

'You say it,' said Kevin.

'Don't get me started.'

'Don't need to.'

'Enough!'

The door that led into the hall banged open and Whistle bounded in, fresh and wet from her bath. She ran around the table, paws clattering and skidding on the tiles, stopped by Aunt Theresa, and shook herself.

'Get that dog outside.'

Grandad opened the door and Whistle ran out as Uncle Rob came in from the hall.

'I hope you cleaned the bath,' said Aunt Theresa.

'Next job on the list,' said Uncle Rob. 'What's going on? I heard Voices.'

40

Aunt Theresa started to explain about the computer and the e-mail but it was becoming difficult to make out the words again, and all he wanted to hear was who the e-mail was from. But they were snapping with their voices, all of them now, and he was holding on to the edge of the kitchen table, and it was as if he wasn't there. So he let go of the table and started to walk round it towards the door into the living room.

'Where are you going?' said his aunt.

'To look at my e-mail.'

'Shower first,' she said.

'Let him read the e-mail,' said his uncle. 'It's from Susan.'

That was his mum. Susan was his mum.

'It's waited all morning. It can wait till he's had a shower.'

'I've got to clean the bath yet.'

'Let the lad read his mum's e-mail,' said his grandad.

'He might have done by now if you'd remembered to tell him,' said his aunt. Then she turned to Nathan. 'Go on, then. But be quick about it. And in the shower straight afterwards. And take off those trainers before you walk on the carpet.'

He took off his trainers and went into the living room.

The computer was on a small wooden desk set

into an alcove near the back window. Nathan sat on the chair in front of the computer, opened the e-mail program, and saw the e-mail from his mum. He clicked it and the e-mail appeared but when he tried to read it the words wouldn't stay in place. They kept moving and shifting on the screen, growing faint then dark then faint again. He shut his eyes but then came the buzzing, louder now, and the black smoke or mist, so he opened them again and stared hard at the screen. He concentrated. The words began to settle and he read them through, trying to sort them into some kind of meaning.

She didn't say much. The weather was bright and cold. It was lovely to see the sea and breathe the sea air. She was starting to relax but she was missing him. *So why hadn't she taken him with her?* There was a harbour and fishing boats and an aquarium with an open top and you could look over the side and see the fish. She'd take him there in the summer. *He wanted to be there now.* And she hoped he was all right and being a good boy and it wouldn't be long before she was back. And then they'd be together again, the two of them.

The two of them.

What about Dad?

He could still hear voices from the kitchen. His aunt and uncle, his grandad, Kevin. Their voices snapping at each other, yapping. No words, just that noise. Snap, yap, snap, yap. It was inside his head and he couldn't think.

What about Dad?

That's what he wanted to write back. His fingers on the keys, tapping out the letters, making the words appear on the screen.

What about Dad? He's down there with you, isn't he? That's why you went there, to meet him. It's where you used to go together. It was your favourite place. You told me. And that's why you've gone there now, that's why you've gone without me. You're going to meet Dad there and you're going to get back together and then we'll all be together again, the three of us.

He read through his mum's e-mail again. The voices came from kitchen. Yap. Snap.

And the buzzing in his head.

He lifted his hand to the mouse and clicked the reply button and then his fingers hit the keys. Tapping out the letters, forming the words.

'Hello, Mum. I'm all right. I took Uncle Rob's dog for a walk today along the canal. I'm glad you're having a good time. Tonight we're having shepherd's pie for tea. But I bet it isn't as good as yours. Grandad showed me some frogspawn in his pond. Joe's coming over here for the day on Monday. I'll see you soon. Love from Nathan.'

He clicked the send button and the e-mail went. Then the screen went black.

He looked at the black screen. Then he leaned down and looked at the unit. It was humming and the light was still on. But the screen was black. He looked at it, the black screen. He should call his uncle, or his cousin, tell them something was wrong with the computer, but he didn't. He just kept on sitting there staring at the black screen.

Staring into the black screen.

From which something stared at him.

It was there, deep down in the blackness of the screen. Something moving. Pulsing, throbbing, like the frogspawn in the pond. He watched it. Twisting and writhing, coiling, uncoiling, turning round and in on itself, as if trying to find a shape. And then starting to rise up through the blackness towards him.

The buzzing was loud in his head, and the black smoke was gathering there, thickening. The tingling was running through his fingers up through his arms and spreading across his whole body, and the black smoke was beginning to fill his head as the writhing, twisting, coiling thing was filling the screen. And now he could see a shape forming, he was starting to make it out, but he didn't know if the shape was inside or outside, in his head or in the screen. And then there was no

44

inside or outside, there was just the shape writhing and twisting and forming itself and the buzzing was in there and the tingling and then it was all just the blackness.

And he was falling into it.

Six

The Cave

Someone is beating a drum.

Slow and heavy, deep, steady. It comes from far off.

She sits in front of the cave. Her legs are crossed, her hands rest on her knees. The cave is near the top of a mountain. The mouth of the cave opens wide in front of her. Where she sits the sunlight glares off the rocks. But inside the cave it's dark.

She cannot see into that darkness.

Far off someone is beating a drum.

Now something is moving in the cave. She cannot see it. She hears it in the darkness, moving. The pad of feet, slow and heavy. Deep, steady. Something coming forward out of the darkness.

Two flickers of light, dancing flame. Eyes looking at her. They come forward. The eyes in a head and thick shoulders behind the head. The head and the shoulders push forward out of the darkness. They are covered in dark fur. And the wide, heavy body that follows the head and the shoulders is too covered in dark fur.

The Bear stands before her. It is a massive creature and its body seems to fill the whole of the cave mouth. Its eyes glitter with a deep light, and there is a deep light too in its dark fur. For a few moments it remains almost motionless, except for a slight rocking of its head from side to side. Then it comes forward slowly from the mouth of the cave and when it is within a few feet of her it stops, and rears up on its hind legs, towering above her, nine or ten feet in height, and the sun blazes from the crown of its head, and its shadow falls across her, and the whole mountain.

The Bear's shadow is a dark river in which she is drowning. A dark shadow that roars in her ears.

And inside that roar, the drum beat, far off.

The roar echoes, fades. The mountain trembles in the light. All is still again, quiet. The Bear drops to its four feet and turns and walks back towards the cave. She hears its voice speak in her head.

'Follow.'

The Bear leads her into the cave. Light from outside splashes across the floor and the walls near the entrance but beyond that all is darkness, and soon she is walking into and through that darkness and she follows the Bear by the sound of its feet padding over the rock. The floor begins to slope downwards and she has to step carefully across its uneven surface and steady herself by pressing her hand against the wall. She can feel the hardness and dryness and smoothness of the rock and knows that the walls of the cave are narrowing and the ceiling is becoming lower, though it must be wide enough and high enough for the Bear to pass through it because she can hear it still padding ahead of her in the dark, just as she can still hear the far off sound of the drum's beat.

Then ahead of her there is light, a low, dull red light, that flickers off the walls and floor and she can see how the tunnel she is walking through drops steeply and at the same time curves to the left and that the source of the light is beyond that curve. She can no longer see the Bear but its voice speaks as if beside her.

'Come.'

Reaching across to press both hands now against the wall to her left, she crouches, and grips her feet into the rock and slides herself down and round to the bottom of the tunnel. And there she finds her-self staring into a high-roofed chamber lit by torch-flames and filled with beasts.

They crowd the walls of the chamber, herds of deer and horses and bison, great cattle with curved horns and humped necks, creatures long gone from her world but living here in the flick and ripple of the flamelight, and she stands among them as they leap and spring and plunge about her, and their hooves thunder in the beating heart of the mountain.

But then she hears a low growl behind her and she turns and the hooves are silenced. There are two wooden torches set in the earth floor of the chamber and squatting between them she sees at first the Bear and then a man robed in a bear's skin and wearing a necklace of teeth and claws. In his hand there is a large stone tool flattened and worked to a point and as she approaches he holds it out towards her, and speaks.

'Dig.'

She kneels and takes the stone tool and begins to scrape at the earth with its point, and soon she has dug a small hole there, and she goes on scraping and digging, making the hole deeper and wider, until at last the point strikes something hard and she stops. She puts the tool down and scrapes away the loose earth with her fingers to reveal a slab of dark rock at the bottom of the hole.

The man speaks to her again.

'Lift the rock.'

She places her fingers beneath one end of the slab and with great effort prises it free of the earth and lifts it upright to fall back and rest against the side of the hole she has dug. And now she sees what has been placed beneath the rock.

It is the skeleton of a man or woman lying on its side with legs drawn up and hands laid beneath the skull. The bones dry and yellowed, scraps of skin, a few strands of hair. Lying in the hole beside the skeleton are a bow, a hide quiver filled with arrows, and a flint knife.

'Take them.'

At the man's words Rasha reaches down into the hole and lifts out first the bow and the arrows and then the knife. The bow is of smoothed and polished ash-wood, and when she takes an arrow from the quiver she sees that its shaft is of the same wood, with a flight of wild goose feathers and tipped with a flint blade. The handle of the flint knife is wound with tightly-bound leather strips. Bow, quiver, arrows, and knife appear newly-made and might have been placed in the grave only yesterday.

'These are your weapons,' says the man, 'as they were hers who now gives them to you.' She looks up at these words into the man's face, and it is a face neither young nor old, dark-skinned and deeply lined, and a savage light in the eyes. 'As you are now so she was once, and as she is now so you shall be. And one day another will come to take these weapons that you give.' Then, in answer to the question she does not speak. 'There is always the creature, and there is always the one who hunts the creature.'

Suddenly, a single drum-beat, loud, close by, and the flames of the torches flare and fill the chamber. The drum-beat again and the man rises to his feet and he is the Bear with arms spread wide and mouth open in a roar. And as the roar shakes the chamber the drum is struck once more and the Bear is a painted image on the wall, one among the many of those fixed and painted beasts. And it is the last thing she sees in that chamber because when the drum is struck again the torch-flames go out and she is plunged into darkness, drowning in that dark river that thunders in her ears. Then comes a cry that might be her own or another's, then a final, heavy drum-beat, and she opens her eyes, and she's sitting in the hut with the drum on her lap, and her hands are resting on the skin of the drum.

In the stone bowl, a dull glow from the fire's dying embers. Lit by that glow, the face of the Old Woman.

She speaks to Rasha.

'You have them.'

On the floor beside Rasha, the bow, the quiver filled with arrows, the flint knife.

'Yes.'

'These are yours now,' says the Old Woman. 'You have their protection and their power. And the power and the protection too of the Bear.'

Rasha closes her eyes for a moment and sees again the Bear standing above her in the flame-lit stone chamber inside the mountain, and the walls filled with beasts. She hears its roar, hears the thunder of hooves. She opens her eyes and looks at the wise and wrinkled face of the Old Woman and knows that she too has seen and heard these things.

'Yes,' she says. 'Now I am ready.'

The Old Woman holds her hands out towards Rasha.

'I will take the drum,' she says.

Rasha lifts the drum from her lap and places it in the Old Woman's hands. The Old Woman looks at the drum for a moment then raises her eyes to meet the girl's.

'There is one more thing you must have,' she says, 'but you will be given that when you make the journey.'

She picks up the wooden bowl and offers it to Rasha.

'Drink.'

Rasha takes the bowl and drinks from it and the water is cool and sweet in her throat. Then the Old Woman takes the bowl from her and empties it on to the floor.

'That is the last you shall have,' she says. 'Your body must be empty so that your spirit can fly easily from it.' Then she stands, holding the drum by her side. 'Now I will go and tell the others that you are ready. They will cut the tree. You will stay here. After three days we shall bring you out of the hut and the tree will be waiting for you.'

She turns and goes to the entrance and draws aside the skin that hangs there. A narrow shaft of sunlight falls across the floor of the hut. She turns to Rasha and looks at her without speaking out of the sunlight and shadow. Then she goes out and lets the skin fall.

Rasha sits alone in the darkness.

Seven

Attic

He was lying down and they were looking at him. They were above him and he could see their faces. They were speaking and he could hear them speaking.

'Nathan.'

That was his name. They were speaking to him. They said it again:

'Nathan.'

'Are you all right?'

'Nathan.'

There were different voices speaking to him and speaking about him.

'He's coming round.'

'Hello, Nathan.'

'What happened?'

'Let him come round.'

'He's come round. His eyes are open.'

'Give him that water.'

'Let him come round.'

'He has. He's come round.'

'Sit him up.'

'Sit up, Nathan.'

Hands lifted him, sat him up.

'Here. Drink this.'

Other hands pressed something against his lips. Water went into his mouth and it was cold and he swallowed it.

'Do you want some more?'

'That's enough for now.'

'Give him some more.'

'Just a sip.'

He drank the water. Then they took it away. Then they were looking at him. And their voices were speaking to him.

'Are you feeling better now?'

'Nathan? Can you hear me?'

'What happened?'

'How are you feeling?'

And then another voice was speaking. He heard it. It was a long way off.

'The screen went black.'

Then they looked at him. And then a voice spoke, close.

'What?'

And then that other voice. And his lips moved as he heard it. It was his own voice.

'The screen went black. But I'm all right now.'

He had fainted. That's what they decided. It was nothing to worry about. He was probably just over-tired. He shouldn't have gone so far along the canal. And having to climb down and get the dog. And being in new surroundings. His aunt was sorry she'd gone on at him. But she hadn't realized. None of them had realized. They should have done. They could phone his mother if he wanted. Did he want them to phone his mother? No, he didn't want them to phone his mother. He was all right, really, he was all right. It was probably best if he went to bed for the afternoon. Try and have a sleep. After a good sleep he'd probably feel better. His aunt would make him some soup. It was tomato soup. Did he want some tomato soup? Yes, he wanted some soup. After some soup and a sleep he would probably feel much better. A good sleep and he'd be right as rain.

After he'd finished his soup and his aunt had taken the bowl and plate away his uncle came in to see him. He told him he'd fixed the screen.

'It's always doing that,' he said. 'One of the wires at the back keeps coming loose. It's OK again now. Till next time.'

'Good,' said Nathan.

'Did you read your e-mail from your mum?'

'Yes.'

'And did you manage to send a reply?'

'Yes. Just before the screen went.'

'Good. She'll want to hear from her favourite son.'

'I'm her only son,' said Nathan.

'I know,' said his uncle. Then he said, 'You OK now?'

'Yes.'

'Sure?'

'Sure.'

'Want anything else?'

'No, thanks.'

'Well, if you do, give us a shout.'

'I will.'

'I'll leave you to it, then.' He reached down with his hand and ruffled Nathan's hair. 'You're my favourite nephew too,' he said.

'I'm your only nephew,' said Nathan.

'I know,' said his uncle.

He dozed for a short time and then he woke and lay in bed looking at his room. It wasn't his room, of course. It was the room he was sleeping in while he stayed with his aunt and uncle. And he was staying with his aunt and his uncle because his mother had gone on holiday to a seaside town in the south-west. And she'd gone by herself. She'd told him she needed a break. The last year had been difficult. It had been difficult for him as well, she knew that. But she really did need this break. She felt frazzled. That was the word she used. Frazzled. She felt frazzled and needed a little time by herself to recharge her batteries. Then she'd come back to him good as new and twice as feisty. That was the word she used. Feisty. She hoped he understood. She asked him to tell her he under-stood. He told her he understood.

But he didn't.

Just like when his mum had tried to explain why his dad had gone and she'd asked him if he'd understood and he'd said he had. But he hadn't.

There was something he understood though.

His mum hadn't gone on holiday to meet his dad. They weren't getting back together. He wouldn't be coming back with her. That was something he'd made up, and made himself believe. But now he knew it wasn't true.

How did he know?

Something told him.

They were talking about him. He'd dozed again and woken thirsty. The glass on his bedside table was empty and he'd taken it and gone along the landing to the bathroom and filled it with water. On his way back he'd heard their voices rising from the kitchen. The door from the downstairs hall to the kitchen was open and by leaning over the rail he could hear some of what was being said.

'I don't think it's anything to worry about.'

'I'm not so sure.'

'She said it might happen.'

'I know what she said.'

'And just to keep an eye on him.'

'That's all very well. While she's off down there.'

'Poor lad. I feel sorry for him.'

'How long's it been going on?'

'Ever since. You know.'

'It can't be right. She ought to take him to see someone.'

'That's up to her.'

'She ought to know. That's what I think.'

'He'll be all right. He's all right now. No point worrying her.'

'Oh, no, mustn't spoil your sister's holiday.'

'Theresa.'

'Well.'

'If it happens again. We'll let her know.'

'You're right. We will.'

There was a shuffle of movement in the kitchen, the sound of a chair being moved, and he stood back from the rail. Then he turned and he was looking at the attic door. In a recess in the wall opposite there were three stairs leading up and the attic door was at the top of the stairs. It was an ordinary door, like into any other room. But this door led into the attic. His house didn't have an attic, not like this. It didn't have a full-sized door leading into the attic like this one. It was just an ordinary door but he was looking at it. And he kept on looking at it.

He slept again and woke and dressed and went downstairs. He said he felt fine now and he sat down to dinner with them at the kitchen table and ate some shepherd's pie. Afterwards they watched television. His aunt and uncle sat on the settee and he sat on the floor and his grandad sat in an armchair and fell asleep. Kevin played a game on the computer and his aunt and uncle kept telling him to turn the sound down or use his earphones. Kevin said that his earphones didn't work. His grandad woke up as if he was surprised he'd been asleep and said he was going to bed and went upstairs. A little while after that he went upstairs to bed himself. As he went upstairs he heard his aunt tell Kevin *one last time* to turn the sound down.

Before he got into bed he took his mobile from his jacket pocket and sent a text to his friend Joe reminding him about coming over on Monday and Joe sent a text back almost straight away saying he hadn't forgotten and he'd be there at ten. He was looking forward to Joe coming over. He wanted to take him over to the Lime Pits and tell him what had happened. They could explore the place together and see if there really was anything there. Joe would listen to him and take him seriously. He was a good friend.

He was lying on his stomach on the bed reading when he heard the door open. He turned over. Kevin was standing in the doorway with his hand resting on the door and keeping it open. Nathan sat up.

'You all right?' said Kevin.

'Yes,' said Nathan. 'I'm fine.'

Kevin didn't say anything and he didn't come into the room. He just stood there in the doorway looking at Nathan. Then he said, 'Do you like it in here? This room?'

'It's all right,' said Nathan.

'It used to be my room,' said Kevin.

'I know,' said Nathan. 'I remember.'

'Before I moved into the room I'm in now,' said Kevin. 'I like that better.'

Then he was silent again for a while, just standing there. Nathan sat in the bed. He felt awkward. When they were younger he'd come sometimes with his mother and father to visit, and once or twice Kevin had taken him out fishing for sticklebacks in the canal with nets. They'd got on all right then. Suddenly Nathan wanted them to get on again, and for things to be like they used to, and he said to Kevin, 'My friend Joe's coming over on the bus on Monday. We'll probably go over to the Lime Pits. Do you want to come?'

Straightaway he wished he hadn't asked him. He'd wanted it to be just him and Joe, so he could tell him about what had happened today. He didn't want to tell Kevin, and he didn't want Kevin to come along with them. He hoped Kevin would feel too grown up to spend his time with a couple of kids.

'All right,' said Kevin. 'Yes.'

'Great,' said Nathan.

'You won't have one of your turns, though, will you?' said Kevin.

'What?' said Nathan.

'One of your turns. Like you had this morning.'

'I don't know what you mean. I don't have turns.'

'What was it, then?'

Nathan didn't know what to say. He wasn't sure what had happened. He remembered the shape in the blackness of the screen, twisting, writhing, growing, taking form, and there came a flutter of panic in his stomach and a tingling in his wrists.

'The screen went black,' he said, 'and then . . . I don't know . . . '

'It was a turn,' said Kevin. 'That's what Mum and Dad said. I heard them talking about it and Mum said it was one of your turns.'

Nathan wasn't looking at Kevin now. He was looking at the quilt on his bed and his knees pushed up under the quilt and his hands resting on his knees.

'It wasn't a turn,' he said.

'You do have them, though,' said Kevin.

Nathan didn't say anything.

'Do you have them a lot?' said Kevin.

He didn't say anything. He stared at his hands gripping his knees raised up under the quilt.

'Only I was wondering,' said Kevin. 'Does it run in your family? Does your mum have them. Or your dad?'

Nathan felt his heart thump.

'Did your dad used to have them?' said Kevin. 'Is that why he left? Was it cos he kept having turns and they had to put him away?'

Nathan looked up now and glared at Kevin. Kevin was grinning. Nathan wanted to hurt him. He wanted to leap off the bed and punch his fist into Kevin's grin. He wanted to see Kevin on the floor crying with his hands clutched over his mouth.

Kevin was grinning.

'Only joking,' he said. He pushed the door wide

63

and turned to go. 'Just make sure you don't have one of them turns over the Lime Pits,' he said. 'Wouldn't want you falling into the pool and drowning.'

The door swung to behind him as he left.

Nathan remained where he was for a minute or so, knees drawn up under the quilt, his hands bunched into fists now on his knees. Then he turned round and thumped the pillow.

The house where his uncle and aunt lived with Kevin and his grandad used to be two houses. One of the houses had been a shop, a small grocery store kept by his grandad and grandmother. His aunt and uncle had lived in the house next door. His grandad and grandmother had lived above the shop. He had a vague memory of visiting the shop when he was very small and being overawed by the high shelves packed with tins and packets and jars, and the strong, deep tangy smell that was a mixture of coffee, tea, tobacco, and sugar. His grandad had given him some boiled sweets in a paper bag. Some years after his grandmother had died his grandad had retired from shopkeeping, and closed the shop, and the wall between the two houses had been knocked down to make one big house. The room he was sleeping in was in the part of the house that had been the shop, and it had been his grandad and grandmother's living room.

That's why it had a fireplace.

It wasn't used as a fireplace any more. A painted wooden screen had been fixed to its front and there was a shelf running across the top. Standing on the shelf was a framed photograph of his grandad and grandmother standing outside the shop. They were much younger and Nathan wouldn't have known who they were if his aunt hadn't told him when she first showed him the room.

The chimney, of course, was still there. If you knocked the wall above the fireplace it made a hollow sound. And behind the fireplace, and the wall where the fireplace stood, was the attic.

Some time in the middle of the night or early in the morning Nathan woke and heard something scratching behind the fireplace. He lay in the dark listening to it. A soft, scratching, rustling sound. He waited for it to stop but it didn't. Then he got out of bed and went over to the fireplace and knelt in front of it. He leaned the side of his head in towards the screen.

Scratch. Rustle.

There was something moving behind the screen.

In the fireplace itself or perhaps higher up in the chimney. Or maybe behind the chimney in the attic. Something small. A mouse, perhaps. Or a bird. A mouse or a bird in the chimney or in the attic.

Then he heard something else. Another sound, harder, deeper. And from further off. A scraping sound, as of something being moved further back in the attic. The sound stopped. Then it came again. A slow, heavy, shuffling sound, like something being dragged across the attic floor.

He sat back from the fireplace.

There was no other sound in the house. Only the rustling and scratching behind the fireplace and the slow, scraping shuffle from the attic.

Then they stopped.

And then he found himself standing up and walking over to the door and opening the door and going out onto the landing. And walking along the landing until he came to the steps leading up to the attic door. He stood at the bottom of the steps looking up at the door and remembered looking at the door earlier in the day. Saying to himself it's just an ordinary door. A door like any other door. And he said that to himself now. It's just an ordinary door.

It's just a bin-liner.

Now he was placing his foot on the first step, and bringing up the other foot, then raising the first foot again onto the second step, and bringing up the other foot again, and now lifting his foot to the third step, and standing on the third step now and there was the attic door in front of him. Then he placed both hands against the door and leaned forward and turned his head and put his ear against the wooden panel.

There was no sound. Nothing was moving or being moved in the attic. Everything was still. He stayed where he was, listening. Then from the other side of the door came the sound of low, soft laughter.

A hoarse voice, whispered laughter. Just a few inches away on the other side of the door.

And then a loud thump.

He stumbled back, staggering, half-falling down the stairs onto the floor of the landing and up against the banister, and the thumping carried on, a fist or the flat of a hand beating against the door, hard and slow and heavy, and he could see the door shaking as it was hit, the doorknob rattling and the panel buckling outwards, beginning to splinter, and he was pressed against the rail of the banister and unable to move, and soon the door would crash open.

He came to on the landing and the dog was barking downstairs. A sharp, yapping bark, and she kept it up, and then he heard someone come out onto the landing and go down the stairs in the other part of the house, and heard his uncle saying to the dog what was it, girl, what was the matter, and his aunt calling down to shut that dog up. And Whistle kept on barking and he could hear his uncle talking to her trying to quieten her, and then she did stop and he heard his uncle going back up the stairs and that was when Nathan went back along the landing and into his room.

He sat on the bed and turned on the bedside lamp. Then got under the quilt and lay on his back.

I was sleepwalking, he thought. I've been sleepwalking before. So it was a dream. The thumping on the door was the dog barking downstairs and that's what woke me up.

But how much of it was a dream? When did he start dreaming?

He lay there with the light on, listening.

There was no sound in the house. It was quiet, and still.

What was the dog barking at?

He listened.

There was a scratching and rustling behind the fireplace.

Something moved in the attic.

Eight

The Bogeyman

When Nathan went downstairs on Sunday morning everyone was out except for his grandad. His grandad told him that his aunt had gone to do her shift in the supermarket and his uncle had taken Whistle out in the car somewhere.

'Probably over to the Chase,' he said to Nathan. 'That's where he usually goes.'

Nathan was disappointed that his uncle had gone without him. He would have liked to have gone over to the Chase too. His grandad must have seen his disappointment, because he said to him, 'He went up to ask you if you wanted to go but he said you were fast asleep. He couldn't wake you. It was early. Perhaps you can go next Sunday.'

'I won't be here next Sunday,' said Nathan. 'Mum's back on Saturday.'

'Oh, yes, that's right,' said his grandad. 'I forgot.'

Nathan asked his grandad where Kevin was.

'He might be still in bed,' said his grandad. 'Or he might have gone out. I don't know.'

And he said it as if he didn't much care either.

His grandad was sitting at the kitchen table with the newspaper and a mug of tea. He asked Nathan if he wanted one.

'Yes, please,' said Nathan.

'And a bacon sandwich,' said his grandad. 'You can't have tea on a Sunday morning without a bacon sandwich. I'd have one with you but I've already had mine. If I have too much it gives me indigestion.' He stood up and filled the kettle with water and plugged it back in and switched it on, and then he opened the fridge and took out the packet of bacon.

'One or two rashers?'

'Two, please.'

He peeled two rashers away from the rest and put them on the grill pan and turned on the grill and put the pan with the bacon on under the grill. Then he went to the bread-bin.

'Brown or white.'

'We have brown at home.'

'We have brown and white here.'

'White, please.'

'And sauce.'

'Yes.'

'Brown or red?'

'Red.'

His grandad took the bottle of tomato sauce out

of the cupboard and put it on the table. By now the kettle was almost boiling and the bacon was cracking and spitting under the grill.

'I used to fry it,' said his grandad. 'But your aunt said I shouldn't. She said it was bad for my heart. So now I grill it.'

'We grill it at home,' said Nathan.

'Everybody does these days,' said his grandad.

When the bacon was cooked his grandad put it on a slice of bread and squeezed a thick splodge of tomato sauce over it and put the second slice of bread on top. He took a knife from the cupboard drawer and cut the sandwich in two and pushed the plate with the sandwich on it towards Nathan. The kettle had boiled and his grandad made the tea in a pot and stirred it and waited a few minutes then poured out some tea in a mug for Nathan and filled his own mug again.

'Two sugars?' he said to Nathan.

'Just one,' said Nathan.

He spooned in the sugar for Nathan and himself then sat back at the table drinking his tea and looking at the newspaper while Nathan ate his sandwich.

'This is good,' said Nathan.

'I know,' said his grandad. 'Nothing like it.'

Nathan sat, eating his bacon sandwich and drinking his tea, and for the first time since he'd come to stay here he felt something like that same warmth and cosiness and ease that he felt at home, without realizing he felt it. He finished his sandwich and drank some of his tea, and then he said to his grandad, 'Grandad, what's in the attic?'

His grandad answered him without looking up from the paper.

'Nothing much,' he said. 'Mostly junk.'

'What kind of junk?'

'The usual kind. Stuff we haven't got round to throwing away. Some of it goes back years. To when I was a boy.' He looked up at Nathan. 'Why do you want to know?'

'I just wondered,' said Nathan.

His grandad kept looking at him.

'Your room's next to the attic, isn't it?' he said.

Nathan nodded.

'It's got the fireplace.'

'Yes.'

'You get noises behind there sometimes. The wind coming down the chimney. Mice, sometimes, and birds. They get in from the attic. Have you heard any noises like that?'

'Yes, I think so.'

'It's nothing to worry about,' said his grandad. 'Mice and birds, that's all.'

Nathan took another drink of tea. Then he said, 'I've heard something else as well.'

'Something else?' said his grandad.

'Yes.'

'What?'

'Like a kind of shuffling sound. Like somebody moving about. It might have been a dream.'

'It probably was,' said his grandad.

'But I woke up,' said Nathan. 'And I still heard it.'

His grandad sat back in his chair.

'You woke up in the middle of the night and thought you heard somebody moving about in the attic,' he said. 'And it scared you.'

'Yes,' said Nathan. There was a prickling in his eyes and he had to blink hard three or four times to keep them clear. 'It's just noises,' he said, and when he spoke his voice felt tight in his throat.

'I know it's just noises,' said his grandad. 'And here and now you know it's just noises. But when you're lying there in the dark listening to them, it's different, isn't it?'

Nathan took his hand away from his eyes and looked at his grandad. He didn't seem to think he was silly. He seemed to be taking him seriously.

'Do you ever hear those noises?' he said.

'I used to,' said his grandad. 'When I was a boy like you. When I first came to live here with my mum and dad. That's your great-grandma and great-grandad. They bought the shop just after the end of the war. That's World War Two. It was old

73

then. And I used to wake up scared nearly every night.'

'What were you scared of?' said Nathan.

'Noises in the night. Creaks on the stairs. Bumps and shufflings. Shadows in the corner. The bogeyman.'

'The bogeyman?' said Nathan.

'It's the thing you're scared of that you haven't got a name for. So you give it a name. I used to call it the bogeyman. Daft name, isn't it?'

Nathan nodded, and grinned.

'But that's all it is,' said his grandad. 'A name. And those noises you hear at night are just that. Noises at night. You understand that, don't you?'

'Yes,' said Nathan.

His grandad drank down his tea then shoved his chair back and stood up.

'Come on,' he said. 'Let's go and have a look.'

'Go and have a look where?' said Nathan.

'In the attic,' said his grandad. 'See if we can find that bogeyman.'

He stood and followed his grandfather out of the kitchen and into the hall and up the stairs. There were two sets of stairs in the house, the one they were climbing now, and another set leading off from another hallway on the other side of the living room. The living room was actually two living rooms knocked into one. Those stairs were in the part of the house that used to be next door to the shop. Nathan and his grandad were climbing the stairs that had been in the shop itself.

They came to the top, and the landing. The landing ran along parallel to the stairs for a short way, then turned at right angles and ran across to the left until it came to a wall with a door in it. On the other side of the door was a similar landing, with the second set of stairs. Nathan's aunt and uncle and Kevin had their bedrooms on that side of the door. Nathan's grandad, and now Nathan himself, had their bedrooms on this side. The attic door was on this side as well.

His grandad climbed the three stairs to the attic door, then stopped, and turned back to Nathan. Nathan was standing at the bottom of the steps.

'All right?' said his grandad.

'Yes,' said Nathan.

'In we go, then,' said his grandad, and turned the door handle and pushed the door open and went into the attic. Nathan could see that it was dark in there, but he heard a click, and saw a light come on. He climbed the stairs then and followed his grandad inside and stood beside him.

'This is it,' said his grandad.

They stood in a long, narrow room, with a slanting roof of rough wooden beams. There was a small skylight high up in the roof, thick with grime.

Hanging down from one of the beams was a light flex with an unshaded lightbulb that illuminated the attic with a glare of bright light.

The left side of the attic was crammed with boxes of all sizes, from large wooden tea chests to cardboard shoeboxes stacked together. One of the tea chests contained Christmas decorations, another was filled with empty glass jars and tin containers. On the right was a jumble of old furniture pushed against the wall. There was a chest of drawers, some dining chairs, a comfortable-looking armchair half covered with a blanket, a large varnished wooden box which, when his grandad opened it, was revealed to be an old record player, and a round wooden table whose top was inlaid with the black and white squares of a chessboard. Most of the squares were chipped and a few were missing.

'I made that table myself,' said his grandad. 'I used to like playing chess. I haven't played it for years.'

He lifted the table and put it to one side, then moved the armchair from where it was pushed against the wall. He knocked on the wall with his knuckles, and there was a hollow sound.

'That's where the chimney is,' he said. 'The fireplace in your room is on the other side, lower down. Look.'

He beckoned Nathan to him then squatted down

beside the wall. When Nathan went across his grandad was pointing to the place where the floor and wall met. There was a small hole in the floorboards there.

'That's where the mice get through.'

'What about birds?' said Nathan.

'Down the chimney,' said his grandad.

He stood up again, wincing a little and pushing one hand into the small of his back.

'Now come and see what's in here,' he said.

A narrow aisle ran between the stacked boxes and the furniture, and at the bottom of the aisle, against the far wall, was an old wardrobe with a cracked mirror set in its door. His grandad walked down the aisle and stood beside the wardrobe. Nathan followed him, and his grandad turned the key that was in the lock and opened the door. Nathan looked inside. It was empty. There wasn't even a single coat-hanger on the rail.

'No bogeyman in there,' said his grandad. He closed the door. 'No bogeyman anywhere. Agreed?'

'Agreed,' said Nathan.

'So what is the bogeyman?' said his grandad.

'Noises in the night,' said Nathan.

'Bumps and squeaks,' said his grandad.

'Yes,' said Nathan.

'And you're not a boy to be frightened of bumps and squeaks,' said his grandad.

77

'No,' said Nathan, and he smiled, and just then he wasn't a boy to be frightened of anything like that. He wasn't frightened of anything at all.

'Right, then,' said his grandad. 'Now that's sorted, let's go and have a cup of tea.'

'We've just had one,' said Nathan.

'You can never have too many cups of tea,' said his grandad.

When they came out of the attic, Kevin was on the landing.

'What you been doing in there?' he said.

'Not much,' said grandad. 'Just having a look.'

His grandad closed the attic door and came down the stairs after Nathan.

'What are you up to?' he said to Kevin.

'Nothing,' said Kevin. 'I've been out. I've just come back.'

'Going to your room?' said his grandad.

'Yes,' said Kevin.

'We're having some tea,' said his grandad. 'Want some?'

'No, thanks,' said Kevin, and he turned and walked along the landing to the door at the end, opened it, and went through to his room.

They went back downstairs to the kitchen and his grandad made another pot of tea. While he was doing that his uncle came back with Whistle, both of them muddy from their walk on the Chase.

His uncle took the dog upstairs and showered her and then he sat at the table and had some tea with them. His grandad didn't say anything to his uncle about the attic. And though Nathan felt better about things he couldn't help wondering why Kevin hadn't used the other stairs to go to his room. And how long he'd been standing there outside the open attic door.

Nine

Spirit Flight

She sits cross-legged on the mat. The mat is woven with patterns and images that tell the history of her people and of the world they inhabit and that world's beginning. Her eyes are closed and there's no movement behind her eyelids. She seems not to be breathing. The bow and quiver of arrows and knife lie beside her on the mat.

She has sat like this for three days, in isolation and in complete stillness. She has eaten no food and drunk no water. Her eyes have gazed outwards through the walls of the hut to the mountains and to the plains beyond the mountains and across the whole world. They have gazed inwards and watched her blood winding its paths through her body, she has seen her heart beating, and she has counted and named each of her bones.

But now the time of fasting and contemplation is over. It is time for her spirit to make its final flight.

She hears her name spoken and when she opens

her eyes she sees the Old Woman kneeling before her. She remains seated as the Old Woman bathes each arm and each leg with water from the bowl, and then bathes her face, and when she has finished she dabs her arms and legs and face dry with a handful of moss. She places the moss in the bowl and puts the bowl down, then takes something from beneath her robe and holds it out towards Rasha.

'Take this,' she says. 'It is the last thing to be given.'

It is a square pouch of animal skin a little larger than her hand and there's a leather thong attached to its corners and something hard and flat and round in the pouch. Rasha puts her hand inside and brings out a disc of black, shiny stone, its edge smooth and its surface so worked and polished it reflects back the image of whatever is put in front of it. She holds it up, being careful not to catch her own face in the disc. She knows that this is the Old Woman's most treasured possession, her most secret and powerful. She places the disc back in the pouch and passes the thong over her head and across her shoulder so that the pouch hangs at her side.

Then the Old Woman stands and goes to the entrance and pulls the hide blanket aside and four women come in.

One of the women is Rasha's mother. The other three are her mother's sisters.

The four women stand at the four corners of the mat on which Rasha is sitting, and when the Old Woman nods to them they squat and take hold of the ends of the poles fixed to the wooden platform beneath the mat and lift it, so that Rasha, still sitting, is raised up between them. Then the Old Woman steps back from the entrance and holds the blanket open as the four women carry the platform with Rasha sitting on it outside.

The bright sunlight hurts her eyes but she does not blink.

The sudden noise hurts her ears but she does not flinch.

It's the sound of singing and clanging bells and wooden sticks struck together, the clamour and noise made by the people who have gathered to see her, but she does not look at them, she looks straight ahead, as they part to make passage for her, and the four women carry her on the platform through the village towards the place where the tree is waiting.

The tree is a tall birch that has been cut down and its branches trimmed and its bark stripped. A pit has been dug for it at the edge of the village and the tree has been placed upright in the pit and the pit filled and packed tight with earth and stones to make sure that it remains upright and does not fall.

The tree is neither living nor dead. It stands between this world and the next. It is the meeting place of these two worlds.

Two smaller trees of ash have also been cut and lopped and stripped and set up on either side of the birch tree, but further back. Strips of woven and coloured thread, blue, yellow, red, white have been wound around the trunks of the three trees, joining them together. The two smaller trees are hung with feathers and skins. But only on the top of the taller central tree has there been fixed a wooden platform like the one on which she is sitting, but larger.

The women lower Rasha to the ground and she stands. Then the Old Woman comes forward and places a robe about her shoulders. It is made of bear skin edged with wolf's fur and hung with an eagle's feathers and the skin of a hare.

'The bear for strength,' says the Old Woman, 'the wolf for cunning, the eagle for sharp sight, the hare for swiftness.'

Then she picks up her bow and quiver of arrows and her flint knife, and slides the knife into her belt and slings the quiver and the bow across her shoulders and steps forward and stands beneath the tree.

The Old Woman raises her arms. The singing and the noise of the sticks and the bells stop. The people stand in silence and in stillness, waiting.

Then Rasha reaches up and takes hold of the lowest stump of branch and hauls herself up and starts to climb.

The tree is about thirty feet high and she climbs it quickly and easily, and when she reaches the top she stands on the platform so that the people can see her and a great cry goes up and the singing and clamour of bells and sticks begin again. She hears it as if from a great distance, as if rising from the plains beyond the mountains, and she feels separate from it and from everything else but the tree. The tree is the only thing holding her to this world. Yet it is also that which will give her passage to the worlds beyond. She understands now what the Old Woman meant when she said that the tree was both end and beginning.

She takes the bow and quiver of arrows from across her shoulder and places them on the platform, and then she lies on her back next to them. The sun is directly above her and its light and heat are fierce and she stares into it without blinking. When she closes her eyes she can see the sun's disc still burning and she feels its light and heat spreading quickly through her body until she is completely filled with them and her body itself is a thing of shining and flame. And through that ocean of fire and light her spirit swims easily and rises to the surface and steps out of her body.

She looks at her body. It lies on the platform with its eyes open. She reaches down and picks up the bow and the quiver of arrows and as she touches them they become flame and light as she is, and the robe across her shoulders shines and is strong with the power of her guardian creatures. She feels their spirits move in her and become one with her spirit, and now it is time and she raises her arms and kicks off from the platform and the tree and the world and takes flight.

Ten

Coming to Get You

After his aunt came back from her shift at the supermarket they went out in the car to a pub for lunch. They took Whistle with them and although the weather was overcast it was mild and they sat outside. By the time they'd come back the afternoon was almost over. He went down to the pond with his grandad to see how the frogspawn was doing but it didn't look any different from the day before. When they went back into the house Kevin was having an argument with his parents about using the computer which ended with Kevin shouting and storming off upstairs and Nathan's uncle going after him to *give him a good talking to*. In the evening they watched television again and then Nathan went up to bed.

The door swung open and he looked up from his book. It was Kevin. As he had done the day before he didn't come right in but stood in the doorway, leaning his shoulder up against the wall and keeping the door open with his hand.

'Still going to the Lime Pits tomorrow?' he said.

'Yes,' said Nathan.

'What we going to do?'

'I don't know. Just look around. I don't think Joe's been over the Lime Pits before.'

'Joe. That's your mate.'

'Yes.'

'What's he like, this Joe?'

'He's good. We're best friends.'

'Is he a laugh?'

'Yes.'

'He don't get scared of things, does he?'

'What kind of things?'

'Anything.'

'I don't think so. No.'

'Not like you.'

Nathan sat. He didn't say anything.

'You get scared,' said Kevin.

'No, I don't,' said Nathan.

'Yes, you do. You're scared of the attic.'

'Who says?'

'You do.'

'I don't.'

'I heard you and Grandad talking,' said Kevin. 'In the attic,' he said. 'Talking about being scared.' He lowered his voice. 'Talking about the bogey-man,' he said.

'There isn't any bogeyman,' said Nathan.

'You think there is.'

'No, I don't.'

'Why are you scared of him, then?'

'I'm not!'

'Scared of the attic,' Kevin said. 'Scared of noises in the night. Scared of the bogeyman. Watch out! He's coming to get you!'

'There's no such thing,' said Nathan. 'There isn't any bogeyman. There's nothing in the attic.'

Kevin grinned.

'That's what you think,' he said.

He went out and the door closed behind him.

Nathan lay back on his bed. After a short while there was a soft scratching of the wood on the other side of the door. He got out of bed and went across to the door and listened.

'Stop it, Kevin.'

The scratching continued.

'Go away!'

A voice spoke low and soft on the other side of the door.

'I'm the bogeyman. I'm coming to get you.'

There came hoarse, whispered laughter.

'If you don't stop it I'll tell your mum and dad.'

The scratching stopped. Nathan waited, listening. He heard footsteps moving away softly across the landing. He waited another minute or so, then opened the door. The landing was empty. But over in the corner, he saw the door between the two parts of the house just closing.

He closed his own door and went back to bed.

He left the light on.

Some time later he woke up. The light was still on. The house was very still and quiet. He thought it must be quite late. He reached over to turn off the lamp. Then he stopped.

Something was moving behind the fireplace. A scratching, a rustling.

'Birds and mice,' he said.

He turned off the light and lay back.

Behind the fireplace, behind the chimney, in the attic, something moved.

Scrape, shuffle, bump. Then again. Scrape, shuffle, bump.

Footsteps dragging.

'There's nothing there,' he said out loud. 'Just noises in the night. There's no such thing as the bogeyman.'

A voice spoke in his head.

It called you.

There's no such thing.

You called it.

There's nothing there.

It came. It's here. It's waiting for you.

There's no such thing there's nothing there there's no bogeyman there's no bogeyman there's no bogeyman.

Coming to get you.

Eleven

The Creature

Here, in this sheltered and silent room.

There, in the dark and still pool.

In both places, and at the same time, it was growing stronger.

In the pool it had a form. And here, now, in the room, it also had a form. And as it had fitted itself to that first form, now it was fitting itself to this other form.

One form for the pool. One form for the room.

Both forms dwelling in darkness and shadow. Both forms creatures of darkness and shadow.

In the pool it writhed its long body and neck and stretched its ragged wings.

In the room it stood in the corner and shuffled across the floorboards.

It reached up to grab with its cold talons.

It scratched at doors and walls with its broken nails.

In the pool it was the Creature, swamp-dweller, shadow-bringer.

In the room it was the Bogeyman, night-walker, shadow-dweller.

Soon it would have another name. When it was stronger.

And it was growing stronger.

Twelve

Rat

Nathan's aunt and uncle lived in an area called Haswich. It was about five miles north of the town where Nathan lived and had once been a mining village. But the mines had long since been closed down and the village had become part of the town. There were blocks of flats on what used to be farm-land and a new estate was being built over the place where the colliery pit-head had stood. But much of the area still had the enclosed feel of a village about it. There were fields nearby, and still the one farm and its surrounding farmland, and there was the canal, and there were the Lime Pits.

Their house was in what used to be the village centre, which was the oldest part. A bus stopped here every hour, taking people into town and bringing them back again. This was where Nathan had arranged to meet Joe when he came over, and this was where Nathan and Kevin waited for him on Monday morning. The bus had been due over five minutes ago and the other people at the bus stop were starting to complain. It was always the same, they were saying. They could never be on time. Sometimes you could be waiting here ten or fifteen minutes. And sometimes they'd just cut a bus without telling you and you'd have to wait a whole hour for the next one.

Nathan was standing by the shelter and Kevin was a few yards away sitting on a wall and drinking from a can he'd bought from the mini-market. He looked as if he didn't want to be seen with Nathan. He looked as if he didn't want to be there at all. Nathan wondered why he was and wished again that he hadn't asked him. He was almost hoping the bus Joe was taking wouldn't turn up. Then they could arrange for him to come another day and this time he wouldn't ask Kevin along.

Joe was grinning when he stepped off the bus.

'It took ages,' he said. 'It went all over the place. And I was sitting next to a bloke who kept talking to himself. Like this.' He made a muttered chuntering noise then laughed and Nathan laughed as well. Then Kevin was standing next to them.

'This is Kevin,' said Nathan, 'my cousin.'

'Hello,' said Joe. Kevin nodded at him. Then Joe said to Nathan, 'Where's this place we're going, then?'

'The Lime Pits,' said Kevin.

'Where are they?'

Kevin was already walking across the road in the direction of the canal.

'Follow him,' said Nathan.

They walked along the canal, the three of them, Nathan and Joe together and Kevin in front. He seemed eager to get to the Lime Pits as quickly as possible, and had hardly spoken a word to them since they left the bus stop. Nathan and Joe had walked together chatting as they made their way along the road to the bridge.

'What's it like over here, then?'

'It's all right.'

'What about your aunt and uncle?'

'I don't know them very well. They're all right, though.'

'Do they do good dinners?'

'Yeah.'

'As good as your mum's?'

'No. My grandad's got a pond.'

'Has he?'

'He made it himself. It's got some frogspawn in it.'

'Wow!'

'You can come back and see it later.'

'Great. Maybe I can put some in a jar and take it home.'

'On the bus?'

'Yeah, on the bus!'

'Yeah!'

But they weren't saying much now. They'd been going along the canal for about twenty minutes and were approaching the brickwork bridge, and the low sky and the grainy light and Kevin's presence had cast a gloom over them that Nathan was trying to shake off. But the more he tried the heavier it felt.

Joe had picked up a stick and was running it along the side of the hedge as they walked and it rattled in the thin and twisted thorny branches. Kevin had pulled his hood up over his head and had his hands shoved into his pockets and his elbows sticking out. He had his knees stuck out sideways too and walked with a kind of side swagger. Nathan hated the way Kevin was walking.

He looked at the canal. A moorhen made a warbled alarm noise and swam out from under the edge nearest to him making its way to a large clump of rushes on the other side. It probably had a nest there. Maybe some eggs. He watched the bird, its head bobbing forward, feet paddling. Moorhens were small birds but they had huge feet. He'd watched one running across some lily pads once. Their feet looked as if they belonged to some other much bigger bird.

The bird was stupid. He thought how stupid the bird was. And then something happened. He watched himself bend down and pick up a large stone and draw his arm back to throw the stone at the moorhen like he'd thrown that one at the crows in the field the other day. Only he was watching himself do it in slow-motion, in a kind of jerky film image that kept stopping and starting. His arm jerked forward and the stone flew jerkily from his hand, stop-starting across the canal, and he wanted to look away but he couldn't, he had to keep watching, as the stone hit the moorhen, and the bird gave a shrill cry, and its body jerked with its wings flapping and its legs thrashing the water, and the water and the canal burst into sharp, ragged pieces flying up.

He looked away. When he looked back he saw the moorhen swimming into the rushes.

Joe was saying something to him.

'Look,' he said.

'What?'

'Look. What's your cousin doing?'

Kevin was standing in the middle of the hump-backed bridge looking at them. His right arm was raised over the top of the bridge and he was holding something in his hand and pointing it outwards over the canal.

'What's he got there?'

'I don't know.'

The air cracked and something splashed in the water near where they were standing. Nathan and Joe looked at each other then ran up to the bridge.

'What you doing, Kevin?'

'What was that?'

'What you got there?'

'Only this,' said Kevin. He held it up so they could see it.

'Is that a gun?'

'No, stupid. It's an air pistol.'

'It's the same thing.'

'No, it's not. This fires pellets, not bullets. Where would I get a gun?'

'Where would you get an air pistol?'

'A mate of mine sold it to me. Really cheap. He collects them.'

'Do your mum and dad know you've got it?'

'No. And they ain't going to. Right, Nathan?'

'Right.'

'Let's have a look,' said Joe.

'OK,' said Kevin. 'Careful, though.'

Joe took the pistol.

'It looks like a real gun,' he said.

'How'd you know what real guns look like?'

'From films,' said Joe.

He looked out over the bridge and raised the pistol and sighted it along the water.

'Can I pull the trigger?'

'If you want.'

'Is it loaded?'

'No.'

Joe squeezed the trigger and the pistol made that cracking sound. Close up you could hear the pop as well. Nathan saw a puff of air spurt from the end of the barrel.

'Can I have a go with a pellet?'

'No,' said Kevin. 'Give it back now.'

Joe gave him the pistol. Nathan said, 'Did you shoot a pellet at us?'

'Not at you,' said Kevin. 'At the water.'

'What if you'd missed the water and hit one of us?'

'I never miss,' said Kevin.

Joe grinned at Nathan.

'He's a real sharpshooter,' he said.

'That's right,' said Kevin. 'I am.' He wasn't grinning. He stuffed the pistol into the large pocket in the front of his tracksuit top. Then he looked straight at Nathan. 'And you,' he said, 'remember, don't say anything about this. Mum and Dad don't know I've got it. And I don't want them to know. Right?'

'Right,' said Nathan.

'Where do you practise?' said Joe. 'Seeing as you're a real sharpshooter.'

'Round my mate's house,' said Kevin. 'He's got a target range set up. And sometimes we go over the fields or come here and shoot birds.'

'What kind of birds?'

'All kinds.'

'Do you hit them?'

'Yes.'

'Even when they're flying?'

'Yes, I told you.'

'I'd like to see you do that.'

Joe was grinning all the time he spoke and Nathan knew what that grin meant. His cousin was beginning to get a pretty good idea what it meant now as well.

'Well, you won't,' he said.

'Why not?'

'Cos I ain't come here to shoot birds today.'

He pushed past them and walked down off the bridge and onto the track that led across the field towards the Lime Pits.

'What you come here to shoot then?' Joe called after him.

Kevin didn't turn his head. He called back.

'I'm going to shoot a rat.'

He was watching them move along the water's edge, stepping over roots, crouching sometimes to peer into the side of the bank, then rising and moving on. Sometimes he lost sight of them as they came to a place where the bank cut inwards, or where the trunk of a tree obscured his vision. Then there would only be the dark water of the pool, and it would draw his gaze deep into it and hold it there so that he could not look away. And it would be as if there was a door opening there at the oozy bottom of the pool and a greater darkness beyond that door into which everything, the earth, the trees, the sky, the pool itself, would fall. Then they would reappear further along the water's edge and from the bank where he stood above he would watch them again.

They were hunting for rats.

Kevin was in front with his air-pistol clutched in his hand, Joe following along behind. Nathan didn't want to go down there with them. He didn't want to be hunting for rats. Kevin had begun to mock him when he'd told them but Joe had said it was up to him, he didn't have to if he didn't want to, and there was something in Joe's voice and the way he spoke that made his cousin give up on his mockery and shrug his shoulders and say OK, and move off down the bank to the pool's edge. Joe had turned to Nathan then and grinned and said, 'Don't worry, we won't find anything. And if we do, he'll miss.' And then he'd followed Kevin down the bank. It was all a game to Joe. Something to laugh about later. He'd have a laugh about it too. They'd make fun of his cousin and his air-pistol and his hunting for rats together.

But he still wished he was able to tell Joe what had happened the other day. It wouldn't be the same telling him some other time. It had to be now and it had to be here. That was the only way it would be real when he told it.

They were still moving along the edge of the pool, and all the time moving further away from Nathan. They were approaching a place where there was a gradual slope down to the water and the bank was thickly grown with trees and bushes. They'd be out of sight completely then. Nathan didn't want to be left on his own so he decided to go back to the path and walk around to where he'd be able to see them. And as he turned to do that a large brown rat came out from under a tree root a few feet away.

He froze. And the rat when it saw him stopped. For a moment the two of them remained as they were, completely still. Then it sat back on its haunches and looked at him.

Its eyes were small and black and there was no fear in them and he could feel them looking at him. The rat's eyes, animal, alien. The creature looking through those eyes animal and alien too.

And not rat. It was something else, something without a name. Something that had assembled rat's bones about itself and tied those bones together with sinew and muscle and cloaked them in rat's skin and rat's fur but it was not rat. Not rat looking at him out of the blackness of those eyes but this nameless something or other. And it was no good him trying to look away from that gaze because it would not let him look away, and it was no good him trying to move because it would not let him move. It had found him out and come for this and would not let him be until it was done.

The eyes looked at him. He saw his image there held and examined.

The eyes looked into him. He felt his image sinking into them.

And then he was looking out through the eyes.

He was the nameless creature wearing rat's skin and rat's bones. He was the nameless ageless thing of no beginning and no end gazing out upon the world onto which it would clamp these rat's teeth and bite and bite through right down to the bone and hold and hold on and not let go. He felt its coiled and quivering power. He felt its strength, growing, deepening, locked fast and rooted in the dark of this earth. And there was something like a wild cry that ran through it, a cry of joy for that strength and that power, and for its being in this world of air and light and blood.

Then it was gone and he was back and the rat was just a rat and it scurried away into the undergrowth and he was standing in front of the tree and the others were climbing up the bank.

He heard their voices.

'If it had come out I'd've had it.'

'If it was there.'

'It was there. I seen it.'

'I didn't.'

'You ain't calling me a liar, are you?'

'No. I'm just saying I didn't see it.'

'Well I did.'

Joe appeared first. He grabbed hold of a branch and pulled himself up onto the top of the bank. Kevin was behind him. Joe was grinning and his hands and face were grimed with mud.

'See any rats up here?' said Joe.

'No,' said Nathan.

'Your cousin says he saw one.'

'I did.'

'Looking at him out of a hole.'

'It wouldn't come out though.'

'I don't blame it,' said Joe, 'with you looking at it.'

'What you mean?'

'I mean it'd be scared, wouldn't it?'

Kevin's hands and face were dirty as well, and his shoes and jean bottoms were thick with mud. He had the air-pistol clutched tight in his right hand.

'It was looking right at me,' he said. 'I could see it. A big one. You could tell. I wish it had come out. I'd've had it. Bam! You'd've heard it squealing then.'

'Why didn't you shoot it while it was in the hole?' said Nathan.

'That's what I told him to do,' said Joe.

'It ain't the same thing,' said Kevin. 'Not like getting it while it's on the run.'

He gripped the pistol with both hands and raised it and pointed it at the ground not far from Nathan's feet. His face was flushed beneath the dirt and blotched with red and there was a fierce light in his eyes. A dark flame burning. He took aim along the barrel and swung the pistol across the ground, following the track of the imaginary rat, and brought it to rest pointing at the root of the tree. Then he raised the pistol and pressed the trigger. There came the crack and pop of the air exploding and the soft thud of the pellet hitting the trunk.

'I don't hear no squealing,' said Joe.

Kevin glanced at Joe then glanced away. He

lowered the pistol. Nathan could still see that dark fury in his eyes.

'Might as well go home,' said Kevin. 'Looks like we ain't going to get any rats.'

'We didn't come over here to get rats,' said Joe.

'Not really,' said Nathan.

'What you come over for then?' said Kevin.

'Mooch around,' said Joe. 'That's right, ain't it, Nate?'

'Yes,' said Nathan. 'Mooch around.'

'So what you going to do now?'

'Don't know,' said Nathan.

'Carry on mooching.'

'You can go home if you want,' said Nathan.

Kevin looked as if he was thinking about it. Then he said, 'What about having a go on the rope?'

The tree they were standing near was the one that had the long rope tied to one of its branches. The branch leaned out over the water and the rope was tied about halfway along, where the branch was thickest. It hung down the slope of the bank and was knotted and looped at its end. Nathan hadn't even noticed it until now.

'It looks dangerous,' said Joe.

'No, it ain't,' said Kevin.

'You ever done it?'

'Course I have.'

'Let's see you, then.'

'OK.'

'I'll hold your air-pistol.'

'No, you won't,' said Kevin, and he lifted his tracksuit top and shoved the pistol in the top of his jeans. Then he slid down the bank until he came to the place where the rope hung down. He took hold of it and gave it a pull. The branch gave a little where the rope was attached and the end that hung over the water shivered.

'Looks dead safe,' said Joe.

'It is,' said Kevin. 'Watch.'

He lifted his right foot and fitted it into the loop and gripped the rope tight with both hands above his head. Then he pushed into the bank with his left foot and swung out a little way from the bank. As he came back he stuck his left leg out behind him and pushed off again from the bank and this time he swung out a little further. He did the same again, and then again, so that soon the swing of the rope was taking him high and far out over the water.

'You reckon he's Tarzan, your cousin?' said Joe.

'Or just a big ape,' said Nathan. Joe laughed.

Kevin was swinging himself forwards and backwards now by bending his knees on the backswing then kicking straight out to take him into the forward swing. As he reached the highest point over the pool he turned his head and called back to them.

'See? Nothing to it!'

'How'd you get back?' Joe called to him.

'Watch!' yelled Kevin.

He was on the outswing again, rising up to the point where he needed to bend his legs for the swing back. But this time, as he reached that point, he twisted the rope round and his body with it so that he was facing them, and freeing his right foot from the loop, he kicked his legs out again so that he swung in high over the bank, and let go of the rope and jumped forward. He landed on the slope of the bank in a crouch putting his arms out on either side for balance, straightened himself, and then climbed up the rest of the slope to stand with them.

His face was even more flushed and blotchy than before.

'Reckon either of you can do that?' he said.

'Not me,' said Nathan.

'I could've guessed that,' said Kevin. He looked at Joe. 'What about you, Nathan's mate?'

'Yes, why not?' said Joe. 'There's nothing to it.'

Nathan watched as Joe went down the bank and reached up and took hold of the rope. He saw him pull on the rope to make certain it was secure, then push his left foot into the loop, but he didn't push off yet, he kept his right foot pressed firmly into the bank as he looked up and made certain of his grip and pulled on the rope again. Nathan knew from the way he did this and the way he'd gone down the bank without looking at him that Joe was nervous but didn't want them to see it. And Nathan felt nervous too. He felt nervous for Joe because he was Joe's friend and also because he knew something was going to happen. And because he didn't know what it was there was nothing he could do about it.

So he just stood on the top of the bank watching as Joe pushed away and out and swung back and pushed away again and swung out a little further and a little higher, and then on the third push he was swinging out high over the water and bending his knees and kicking to carry himself higher and further each time. And he knew that Joe wasn't nervous any more, he was lost in the rush and the thrill of the swing and the feeling of his body in flight through the air. As he swung out and up again to the highest point, Joe wrapped his legs around the rope and stood one foot on top of the other and pushed himself up straight and as he began the swing back he turned himself round to face them and came back towards them holding on with one hand and with an arm thrust out and his mouth open and a cry coming out of it.

'Woo—woo—wooooooooo!'

And as he swung up and over the bank he was

laughing in their faces and then grabbing on with both hands again and twisting himself round and bending his knees and kicking out with his legs to take him back over the pool.

'He's enjoying himself, your mate, ain't he?' said Kevin.

Nathan heard him and did not hear him. The words and the voice that made the words were there, but there was something beyond them or deep inside them that seemed to be part of the unknown thing that was going to happen, and that he could feel getting ready to happen, winding itself tight and tighter still around the pool and Joe swinging out over the pool and Kevin's words spoken low and soft. And around himself too. Himself at the centre of that winding and tightening. A cold wire pulling itself through his body.

Joe was coming back with one arm flung out again, heading towards the bank and the twist and the turn and the kick outwards. Nathan was watching him, and then suddenly he felt other eyes watching him as well. He turned and looked at Kevin. His cousin's gaze was fixed on Joe. His head was pushed forward and his mouth set fast. And the fierce light was still in his eyes. The dark flame burning darker. Not in Kevin's eyes. In the thing that stared out through Kevin's eyes. The same thing that had stared out through the rat's eyes. That nameless creature, the alien other, gazing towards Joe and drawing Joe towards it with that gaze. Joe's image held fixed in its flame. Nathan knew it because Nathan felt it. He felt the fury and the rage of the creature that was inhabiting Kevin, felt a thrill too, and a wild joy that possessed it and possessed him, terrifying and wonderful. He gasped with the shock of it.

And with the shock of a sudden glimpsed understanding.

The dark flicker of flame in Kevin's eyes and the rat's eyes. The writhing shape in the blackness of the computer screen. The flicker of blackness twisting in the sky above the pool. They were the same thing.

The pool was an eye staring up at Joe.

The wire was winding tighter. There was a buzzing in his head, there was a dark mist gathering.

A voice spoke out of the darkness.

You called it.

He spoke back to the voice.

No.

And as if in answer Kevin raised the air-pistol, gripped in both hands, and aimed it towards Joe.

'No!'

Nathan cried out and at the same time ran forward and pushed hard at Kevin's shoulder. Kevin stumbled sideways off balance. He kicked out with his foot trying to regain his balance but his other foot slipped in the mud and he tumbled sideways and backwards onto the ground. He stared up at Nathan in shock and outrage.

'What you doing!'

'What were you doing?'

'Nothing!'

'You were going to shoot him!'

'I wasn't!'

'I saw you! You had your pistol. You were aiming at him!'

Kevin pushed himself up to his feet. He held the air-pistol out towards Nathan. Its barrel was pointing directly at his face. He heard Joe give another long cry as he came swinging back in.

'It ain't loaded!' said Kevin.

'What?'

'I was just messing around! There ain't no pellet in it! Look!'

He pressed the trigger. Nathan flinched back as the pistol cracked and the air snapped at his cheek and at the same time the wire that was being pulled through his body snapped free and out. Then he heard Joe's cry and it wasn't the cry of before and he turned to see the rope swinging loose and Joe dropping into the water.

'Bloody hell! He's fallen in!'

Nathan and Kevin scrambled down the bank as

Joe went under and by the time they reached the bottom he was coming up again spluttering and thrashing with his arms at the water.

'He'll be all right. He ain't far out.'

And it looked as if he would be all right because he was starting to swim towards the shore and he knew that Joe was a strong swimmer and he called something out to him, but afterwards he couldn't remember what, because as he called out Joe seemed to twist in the water and his arms flew up as if he was trying to grab hold of something and then he was gone.

Thirteen

Mobile

They were staring at the water. There were ripples spreading out from the place where Joe went under. The rope hung down loose and straight from the branch.

'We've got to do something.'

'What?'

'I don't know. Something.'

'What though?'

'Go in after him.'

'Are you crazy?'

'We've got to!'

'You'll drown as well.'

'He's not drowned.'

'Phone somebody.'

'He's not.'

'My phone! I left it on charge.'

'He's not coming up.'

'Have you got yours?'

'What?'

'Your phone.'

'Yes. Here.'

'Phone somebody.'

'Who?'

'Emergency. 999.'

'How they going to get here?'

'I don't know. Just phone.'

Then it didn't matter about phoning anyone because as suddenly as he'd gone Joe was up again and thrashing at the water like before and then swimming hard and fast towards the shore.

'Joe!'

Nathan stepped into the water and reached out his hand as Joe found the bottom with his feet and waded out of the pool, and he grabbed hold of Joe's arm and pulled him up onto the bank.

'Joe. Are you OK? Joe?'

Joe was coughing and spitting water and pulling weed from his hair and eyes and he wasn't looking at Nathan or Kevin, and he didn't seem to hear them or even know that they were there.

'What happened?'

'He fell in, that's what happened.'

'I mean when you went under. How come you went under like that?'

Now Joe did look at Nathan but he still didn't say anything. He shook his head and pushed past Nathan and Kevin and began to scramble up to the top of the bank.

'What is it about this pool you and your mates like falling into it?' said Kevin.

Nathan ignored Kevin and followed Joe to the top of the bank. He was sitting hunched forward on a large root and he was shivering. Water was still running off his soaked clothes and making a puddle in the earth at his feet. Nathan stood beside him.

'We'd better get back,' he said. He felt all right now and his mind was clear. 'Back to ours. You can have some of my clothes. We'll just tell them you fell in. We won't tell them about swinging on the rope.'

He was talking and Joe wasn't listening. He was sitting on the root and shivering and the water was dripping.

'Nor about my air-pistol,' said Kevin. 'We won't tell them about swinging on the rope or the air-pistol.'

'Right,' said Nathan. He looked again at Joe.

'You ready, then? Shall we go? We'd better go.'

Joe didn't move.

'He stinks,' said Kevin. 'Worse than you did when you fell in.'

'Shut up, Kevin,' said Nathan.

'Don't tell me to shut up!' said Kevin. He stood close in front of Nathan. 'You pushed me over. I ain't forgot that.'

'You know why I did.'

'Yeah, cos you're a prat.'

Nathan stood his ground. He wasn't going to move. He stared at Kevin and didn't take his eyes away. He wasn't sure what Kevin was going to do. They stood facing each other. Then Kevin turned away.

'I'm going,' he said, and walked through the undergrowth and out onto the path. 'I ain't hanging around for you two.' He started walking off along the path. He called back. 'I'll tell Mum what happened. Not about the rope. And you don't tell about the air-pistol.' Then he was gone.

Nathan turned back to Joe. He was sitting as before, crouched with his arms on his leg, staring ahead.

'Joe.'

This time Joe heard.

'Yes, OK,' he said. 'In a minute.' Nathan stood waiting. Then Joe spoke again. 'Something pulled me down,' he said. 'I come up and I started to swim and then it grabbed me and pulled me down.'

'What did?'

'I don't know. Something. I felt it. It grabbed me and pulled me down.'

He sat on the root, hunched forward, staring ahead, shivering.

When they got back his aunt was waiting for them. Her shift at the supermarket wasn't until the evening. She'd run a bath for Joe and while Joe had a bath she put his wet clothes in the washing machine and Nathan found some of his clothes for Joe to wear. She'd already had a go at Kevin and now she had a go at Nathan and said what did he think he was playing at, that was twice now he'd been over to that place and twice he'd got himself in a mess, and their house in a mess too, walking mud in everywhere. And she wanted to know how it happened, anyway, how did his friend manage to fall into the pool, and Nathan said he wasn't sure, they were just playing and Joe slipped and fell in. And his aunt said well, that was it, no more going over there, did he understand, and he said yes, he understood, he promised he wouldn't go over there again, and she said he'd better not.

Then Joe came down in Nathan's clothes and thanked Nathan's aunt, and she made them some sandwiches and called Kevin to come and get something to eat, but he didn't come down, he was sulking, she said, because she'd given him what for. Well, it was his own fault if he missed his lunch, he could go hungry as far as she was concerned. Then she asked Joe if there was anyone at home and he told her yes, his dad was, so she asked Joe for his home number and then went into the living room to phone Joe's dad because he ought to know what had happened. And while she was out phoning Nathan asked Joe to tell him again about being pulled under the water.

'It's like I told you,' said Joe. 'Something grabbed me and pulled me down.'

'What was it?'

'I don't know, do I? I didn't hang around to look.'

'Then it let you go.'

'Well, yeah. Or I wouldn't be here.' He took a drink of tea. 'I'm not making it up.'

'I know you're not,' said Nathan. Then he said, 'Was it like fingers?'

'Fingers?'

'Fingers round your leg.'

Joe looked at Nathan.

'Yes,' he said. 'Like fingers.'

'Cold fingers, holding tight.'

'Yes,' said Joe. 'How do you know?'

Nathan was going to say something. Then his aunt came in. She'd phoned Joe's dad and told him what happened and his dad was coming over straight away in the car to take him home. His clothes would be washed by then but they wouldn't be dry so she'd fold them and put them in some plastic bags and he could take them with him and put them out to dry when he got home. Nathan didn't have a chance to talk to Joe again because his aunt stayed in the kitchen sorting out Joe's wet clothes and by the time that was done and she sat down and had a cup of tea Joe's dad had arrived and he came in and they had to tell him again how they'd just been playing about and Joe had slipped and fallen in and he was OK he just got wet, that's all. Then Joe's dad apologized for all the trouble Nathan's aunt had been put to and thanked her for washing his clothes and he took the bags and he and Joe went outside to the street where the car was parked. Nathan went with them and waited as Joe got into the car next to his dad and waved as they pulled away and watched the car drive off down the road and stood there watching until it was gone.

He lay on the bed in his room. His aunt and his cousin were arguing downstairs. Their voices grew louder but he still couldn't make out what they were saying. Then he heard the front door open and his aunt shouted something and his cousin shouted something back and the front door slammed shut. He heard his aunt go into the kitchen and turn the radio on.

A little while later there was a knock on the

bedroom door. He said, 'Come in,' and the door opened and his grandad stood there. His grandad had been in the garden when they'd come back from the pool and he hadn't come into the house.

'I hear you've been in the wars,' his grandad said.

'Not me really. It was Joe.'

'Your friend.'

'Yes.'

'He fell in the pool.'

'Yes.'

'It can be dangerous over the Lime Pits,' said his grandad. 'People have drowned in that pool. You have to be careful.'

'I know,' said Nathan.

'But you won't be going over there again.'

'No.'

'Your aunt made that plain enough,' he said. 'I've heard the whole story. And been given my orders.'

'Your orders?'

'She's on an all-day shift tomorrow. I'm to make sure you don't go over.'

'Don't worry, grandad. I won't. I don't want to go near the place again.'

'I'm sure we can find something to amuse you here. Have a rummage around, see what we can come up with.'

Nathan smiled. He liked that word, *rummage*.

'It must be a bit difficult for you, staying here,' his grandad said.

'It's all right,' said Nathan.

'It's not home though, is it?'

Nathan shook his head.

'Never mind. It won't be long now till your mum's back. A few days.'

He nodded.

'I suppose you're missing her.'

He nodded again.

'And—' His grandad stopped. Whatever he'd been going to say, he changed his mind about it. 'As I say, it won't be long.'

He stood in the doorway for a minute not saying anything. Nathan wanted to say something to him but he didn't know what. Then his grandad said, 'Right, then. I'll leave you to it.'

Nathan smiled again.

'I'm looking forward to having a rummage around tomorrow,' he said.

'There's nothing like a good rummage,' said his grandad. 'As long as you keep stopping for a cup of tea.'

'Nothing like a cup of tea,' said Nathan.

Now his grandad smiled. 'You're catching on,' he said. He turned to go, then stopped, and turned back.

'No more bad dreams?' he said. 'No more bogey-men?'

'No,' said Nathan.

'Good,' said his grandad. 'That's it.'

Then he left.

Nathan watched the door close. He knew what his grandad had been going to say when he'd stopped. He knew what the 'And—' was. 'And you miss your dad.' Nathan was glad he hadn't said it.

Some time after his grandad left he got up and fetched his rucksack from the corner of the room. He took out an exercise book and his pencil case and took a pencil from the case. Then he sat on the bed with the exercise book and pencil and started to write down a list of all the things that had happened since Saturday. His mother had told him that if things are troubling you it's a good idea to write them down. It's a way of putting your troubles outside yourself, she'd said. Then you can look at them, and see which ones are really troubling you, and which ones aren't. And you can start to deal with those that are. You can take control.

They'd done that together after Dad had left.

He wrote slowly, making his handwriting as neat as he could, and put each thing on a separate line, with a space between the lines, so that he could read them more easily. When he'd finished he put the pencil down and read the list out loud to himself.

'I saw something large and black in the sky above the Lime Pits. Then it dropped down through the trees.

'It wasn't a crow and it wasn't a bin-liner. I don't know what it was.

'Something made Whistle bark and she went down to the side of the pool. When I went down there after her I felt like there was something watching me out of the pool.

'I put my foot in the water without knowing it and something grabbed my foot.

'I saw something in the computer screen when it went black. It was like the thing I saw in the sky above the trees. It was like looking into the pool.

'I heard something moving about in the attic.

'There's a voice speaks in my head.

'There was something looking at me out of the rat's eyes that wasn't the rat. And the same thing was looking out of Kevin's eyes when he was aiming the pistol at Joe.

'Joe said something grabbed hold of him when he fell into the pool and pulled him under. Joe doesn't make things up like that. I think it was the same thing that grabbed me.

'I think the thing that I saw in the sky and the thing in the pool that grabbed me and the thing that I hear moving in the attic is the thing that speaks and it's the same thing.'

He put the exercise book down on the bed and thought about what he'd written. He knew it was real. He knew he wasn't imagining these things and making them up. He knew what making things up felt like and this wasn't the same. This felt real.

But writing it down wasn't enough. He still needed to talk to someone. He'd lost his chance with Joe. The only other person might be his grandad. But he wasn't sure about him. The way he'd spoken about the noises in the attic. They were just noises, that was all. Nothing to be afraid of.

His grandad was wrong.

His mum would listen to him. But she wasn't here. So would his dad. But he wasn't here either. He hadn't been here for over a year and he didn't know if he'd ever see him again.

And he still didn't know why.

When it had first happened he'd cried and shouted and then he'd stopped crying and shouting but the angry and hurt feelings hadn't gone away. They were still there, and he just carried them around inside him now. And sometimes it felt as if they were outside him too, and he was having to push his way through them, like pushing his way through some kind of dark and heavy mist that pressed around him and against him and he couldn't get free of it.

He picked up the exercise book again and read what he'd written.

When he was younger he'd had a dream. In the dream he was being chased by a tiger along the streets where he lived. He was terrified and he ran as fast as he could but he could hear the tiger behind him getting closer. Then he tripped and fell and rolled over onto his back and the tiger was on him, its forepaws pressed into his shoulders holding him down. He saw the tiger's face huge and golden and black with its golden and black eyes gazing down at him. The tiger's face was all he could see and he was no longer frightened. Then the tiger spoke to him.

'If you didn't run I wouldn't chase you.'

Then he'd woken.

He'd never forgotten the dream and it came back to him now as clear as it had been when he'd dreamed it.

If you didn't run I wouldn't chase you.

All right, he thought. I'll stop running. And I'll look you in the face.

He closed the exercise book and put it back in his rucksack and put the pencil back in the case and put that in the rucksack as well. Then he went out of the bedroom and along the landing until he came to the steps that led up to the attic door. He stood at the bottom of the steps looking up at the door. His heart was beating fast and his mouth was dry but there was no tingling or buzzing and he felt all right. His head was clear. So he climbed the steps and turned the handle and pushed the door open and went in.

The first thing he did was turn on the light. He stood with the open door behind him looking at the attic. It was the same as when he'd been in there yesterday with his grandad. The stacked boxes on the left and the old furniture piled together on the right. The aisle running in between. And down there at the end of the aisle, pushed against the wall, the wardrobe with the mirror on its door. He could see himself in the mirror, a small figure standing a long way off.

The harsh light from the bulb showed up all the edges and angles, the tattered and frayed corners, the tears in the upholstery, the faded patterns and the dust. It showed up the stillness. He was the only living thing in the attic and he felt strong.

He walked down the aisle to the other end of the attic until he stood in front of the wardrobe. His reflection in the mirror looked back at him. He pulled a face at it. He pulled his mouth wide with his fingers and stuck out his tongue. Then he turned the key in the wardrobe door and pulled it open. There was nothing inside. He closed it and turned the key again. Then he turned and walked back up the other end of the aisle and before going out he turned and took one last look at the attic. Then he switched off the light and went out and shut the attic door.

And then the voice spoke.

Brave boy. But I'm no tiger. And I'm not ready yet.

That evening his mother phoned. His aunt had gone for her evening shift and his uncle was back from work and watching television. Kevin was back too from wherever he'd stormed off to and was playing a game on the computer. His grandad was sitting at the table in the kitchen reading a book about garden birds. He took the phone into the hall and spoke to her there.

The first thing she asked him was if he'd received her text.

'No,' he said. 'When did you send it?'

'This afternoon,' she said.

'I didn't hear my phone,' he said.

'Perhaps you had it turned off,' she said.

He asked her what she'd been doing and she told him and then she asked him how he was and if everything was all right. He told her everything was fine and then told her about Joe falling into the pool.

'He fell in? What do you mean?'

'He fell in.'

'How did he fall in?'

'We were just playing around and he slipped off the bank and fell in.'

'Right in, do you mean?'

'Yes.'

'Is he all right?'

'Yes. He just got wet.'

'You didn't fall in as well, did you?'

'No.'

'Are you sure?'

'I'm sure. I didn't fall in. I got a bit wet helping Joe out. Just my trainers, that's all.'

Then he told her about taking Joe back to his aunt's house and lending Joe some of his clothes and his aunt washing Joe's clothes, and he made it all sound like a bit of fun, a lark, with no harm done, and he felt bad about it because he knew he was lying and he could hear the edge of concern in his mum's voice when she spoke to him.

'I bet that pleased your aunt Theresa.'

'She wasn't too happy.'

They both laughed.

'Mind you, I don't blame her,' his mum said.

Then she said, 'I don't think you should go over there again, Nathan.'

'Don't worry, mum. I won't. Aunt Theresa said I can't. And I don't want to anyway.'

Then he changed the subject by asking her about the text she said she'd sent him, and she told him it wasn't important, just a daft text, and he said he'd go and have a look at it after they'd rung off. Then there wasn't much more to say, and she told him once more to be careful and that she missed him and she'd be seeing him soon and then she rang off.

He went upstairs straight away to look at the text. He looked in the pockets of his jacket for his mobile but it wasn't there. Then he looked in the bed and under the bed, and he emptied everything out of his rucksack and searched the whole room but he couldn't find it. He went downstairs and looked in the kitchen and the living room but he didn't tell his grandad or his uncle that he was looking for it because already he knew where it was and what he'd have to do to find it again. He told his uncle he was going up to bed and said goodnight to him, and to his grandad.

After he'd searched the bedroom one more time he went to the bathroom and cleaned his teeth then went back to his bedroom and undressed and put on his pyjamas and got into bed and lay there with the light on. He was trying to think of a way of going back to the Lime Pits without anyone finding out. He remembered taking his mobile out of his pocket when Joe had gone under the water and knew that he must have dropped it there when Joe came up again and he went to help him out. He only hoped he hadn't dropped it in the water.

It won't take long, he thought. I'll go to the place where Joe fell. If it's there I can get it, and if it's not I won't look for it and come straight back. I'll take Whistle with me. It'll be all right. It won't take long.

He lay with the light on, picturing every step of the journey there, climbing down the bank, seeing the mobile lying on the bank by the water, picking it up, climbing the bank again, and coming back along the canal. He went over it and over it until it was real, and it was the only way it could happen.

His aunt came back from her late shift. The doors were locked, the lights turned off. Everyone went to bed. The house was still. He turned his light off.

He lay awake, thinking about going to the pool.

He lay awake, waiting for the noises to start. He lay awake for a long time.

Then the noises started.

Fourteen

The Other World

She's awake. Her eyes are open. She's looking at the other world.

There are trees and there are shadows between the trees. There are branches and bushes and buds on the branches and buds on the bushes ready to open. There's a smell of earth and bark and old leaves in the earth. Cold air. A pale light.

She turns over and sits up and pulls a face. Her legs are covered in scratches and one scratch is long and deep and a trickle of blood runs from it. Her hands are covered in scratches as well. She touches a finger to the blood and lifts it to her mouth and tastes it. The blood is real.

Her bow lies next to her on the earth and the quiver of arrows. Some of the arrows have fallen out of the quiver. She pushes herself to her feet and picks up the fallen and scattered arrows and puts them back in the quiver then slings the quiver over her shoulder and picks up her bow. Neither the bow nor the arrows nor the quiver shine with golden light. Her robe is heavy on her shoulders and its fur in places is caked with mud and there's a tear in one of the shoulders. An eagle's feather hangs loose. She pulls it off and puts it in her belt next to her knife.

The black stone disc is still in its pouch. She puts her hand inside the pouch and runs her fingers over the hard smooth surface of the disc. She feels its secret warmth and magic.

Then she takes her hand out and looks up at the tree from which she has fallen.

When she first came into the other world she was in her spirit body which still burned with fire and light and she came to rest on the highest branch of the tree and if anyone had been there they would have seen only a brightness shimmering as if a ray of the sun had broken through the clouds to fall upon and illuminate the tip of that branch. And she saw the world itself through those glimmering flame-shot spirit eyes, quivering and uncertain and ghost-like, a place of strangeness, and shifting trembling forms.

Then she breathed.

And she felt the whole weight of the world fall upon her, and she staggered beneath it, her bone and her blood, and trapped and entangled by her own flesh, she fell.

And for a while lay in darkness and then woke.

And now she is here in the other world. And the other world is real now and she is in it.

She remembers what the Old Woman said to her. She closes her eyes and hears her voice speaking the words.

'You must seek out the Creature. Track its path. Hunt it. You must discover the form it has taken. And in that form you must kill it. You cannot return until you have killed it. If you do not kill it you will not return.'

She shivers and pulls her robe about her to feel its warmth and also the warmth of her guardian creatures. Bear and wolf and eagle and hare. She feels them close. She feels their power and their knowing, their strength and their cunning. They are here with her and she is not alone.

Near to where she stands there is a ditch and a stream running through it. Carrying her bow in one hand she follows the stream on a track that runs along the top of the ditch, and track and stream wind through the trees until the track drops and bends to the left and the stream runs under the track, and she's out of the trees facing a bare field. There are crows in the field and a dull light. The sky above the field is grey with cloud.

The field slopes upwards and the track continues across the field and she walks along the track until she comes to a place where the field ends and there's a line of leafless bushes running along its edge and a gap in these bushes where the track cuts through and leads up to a bridge. The bridge crosses over a waterway which is like a river but its sides are cut straight and the water is not running but still. She climbs the track and stands on the bridge. In the distance she can hear a low rumble as of thunder and a storm approaching but the rumble is continuous and neither the light nor the sky is stormlike. The noise has no meaning for her and she ignores it.

She looks down from the bridge into still water, then she looks up and along the course of the waterway and scans the fields to its left and to its right, and lifts her eyes to the skyline and lets her gaze run across it and then brings her gaze round until it comes to rest on the wood at the bottom of the field from which she's just walked. She lifts her gaze to the spiked tops of the tree then lifts it higher until it comes to rest on a patch of sky above the wood.

It is grey and flat like the rest of the sky with nothing to set it apart but her eyes fix on it and remain fixed. Keeping her gaze there she reaches into the pouch and takes out the disc. She cups it in her hand and raises it until it's level with her eyes, then angles it round and up so that it's facing partly towards the sky and partly towards her so that by turning her head she will be able to see what's reflected in its surface.

She turns her head and looks.

There are the tops of the trees and the sky above the trees, glowing as if lit by fire in the polished sheen of the disc's surface. And in the sky a black shape twists and turns like a length of ribbon caught and carried by the wind. The nape of her neck prickles and there's a bristling of the fine dark hairs that grow there. She looks away from the disc towards the patch of the sky and it's clear. But in the disc the shape still writhes above the tree tops.

And then there's something else as well. She catches the briefest glimpse of it at the disc's edge furthest from her. She turns the edge a little closer in towards her face and suddenly there are two eyes looking out of the disc. She moves the disc further away and sees in the surface the face of a boy and the boy is staring not at her but at something beyond her and above.

She brings the disc in again and turns the edge out towards the sky above the trees and once more sees the dark shape there, but almost immediately it begins to snake downwards towards the trees and then it disappears in and among them and the sky is empty both in the surface of the disc and the outer world.

She puts the disc back into the pouch and makes her way at a jog off the bridge and back down the track across the field towards the wood.

When she reaches the wood she does not stop but carries on at the same pace along the track as it crosses the stream and then rises to run alongside and above it and goes on following the track, past the place where she fell from the tree, until it comes to a place where the stream runs under the track again and opens out into a wide pool. She stops here and looks up at the opening in the trees above the pool where the grey sky shows and then down at the pool itself where that same sky is reflected. She takes out the disc and holds it towards the water and looks at the reflection of the water in the disc's surface. Then she raises the disc so that it reflects the island and the pool beyond the island where it lengthens and narrows and disappears among high banks thickly grown with trees and bushes.

Once more she puts the disc back and jogs off along the path around the edge of the pool until she comes to the far side and stands on a high bank dropping down almost sheer into the water.

She stares down into the black water. Then she puts down her bow and takes off her quiver and lays that down beside the bow and takes off her robe as well and places that over the bow and the quiver. Then she takes hold of a low hanging branch and eases herself over the side and lets go of the branch and slides down the bank to the bottom. Now she's standing at the water's edge and she takes out the disc once more and crouches low over the water and holds the disc so that it's face down towards the pool.

Something flickers across the shining surface of the disc.

Her neck hairs stiffen.

Then she turns her head and looks into the disc and sees the Creature.

Fifteen

Mad Dog

He stood on the brickwork bridge getting his breath back and looking down towards the wood. He'd run all the way along the towpath from the bridge by the road, with Whistle running alongside, yelping sometimes with excitement. It was mid-morning. He'd left the house at around ten-thirty. His grandad had been getting ready to have a nap, and wouldn't wake from it till lunchtime. He was sure he could be back before then. His aunt wouldn't be home till much later. Kevin had gone out earlier in the morning to a friend's house. Probably the friend who had all the air-guns. To shoot at targets or sparrows.

Whistle was snuffling at the metal gate that led to the farm. Nathan went over to her, took the lead from around his neck and clipped it to her collar. He didn't want to risk her running off and losing her again. He scratched behind her ear.

'Come on, girl,' he said. 'Let's go.'

Then with the dog beside him he walked off the

bridge and down onto the track, and set off across the field towards the Lime Pits.

He'd got up early and had breakfast with his grandad. While they'd been having it Kevin had come into the kitchen and taken a slice of toast from the plate and ate it standing up and then told them he was going out to his friend's. He'd said he'd be out all day. Then he'd gone. He and his grandad had finished their breakfast, then washed up and dried the plates and cups, and then his grandad had suggested they went down to the pool to see how the frogspawn was getting on. He'd felt uneasy about going down there after what had happened last time but it had been all right. He and his grandad had crouched by the side of the pool and his grandad had lifted the netting and he'd looked at the frogspawn and nothing had happened. He'd just been there looking at frogspawn.

'Look,' his grandad had said. 'They're starting to change.'

Nathan had looked closer and seen that the black specks inside the shiny eggs were bigger now, each one nearly filling out the whole egg, and a few hadn't been round any more but oval shaped, with one end fatter than the other.

'They'll start to develop pretty quickly now,' his grandad had said. 'You'll have to come back and check up on them.'

'I will,' he'd said.

After that he'd helped his grandad bring out the potted plants he'd kept in the greenhouse during the winter and place them around the garden, because the weather was warming up now, his grandad had said, and they'd be better off outside. Then they'd pulled up some of the weeds that had started to grow around the garden plants and dug over the compost heap and then his grandad had said that was enough for now and they'd gone inside for a cup of tea.

As his grandad had been settling down for his morning nap Nathan had told him he was going to take the dog for a walk.

'Where?' his grandad had said.

'Just along the canal.'

'You won't go to the Lime Pits?'

'No. I'll just take her as far as the bridge and then we'll come back.'

'All right, then. Don't be too long.'

'I won't.'

Then his grandad had settled down in his chair with the radio on and he'd put his coat on, called Whistle and put the lead on her, and set off for the canal.

141

He felt bad about lying to his grandad but there'd been nothing else he could do. He had to go to the Lime Pits and try and find his mobile.

That was the only reason he was here.

There was no other reason.

It took no time at all to enter the wood and make his way along the path that led around the pool to the place where the rope hung down over the water. The place was quiet and still. Hardly any movement except for his own and the dog's. His feet crunching on the gravel. Whistle trotting along beside him. There was no sense of anything unusual. No presence in the shadows. No eyes watching him. He didn't think about what had happened there the day before or on the Saturday when he'd first gone there. He was trying hard not to think about anything.

He stood on the edge of the bank and looked down. He couldn't see his mobile anywhere. But there were roots and hollows down there and clumps of undergrowth and he was going to have to go down there and look. But he didn't want the trouble of taking the dog down with him so he held on to her collar with one hand and unhooked the lead then passed it around the trunk of a silver birch tree that grew close to the path. Still holding onto the collar he managed with one hand to thread the hook through the hand loop so that the lead was fastened around the trunk and then he hooked the lead to the collar again. It didn't leave much space for Whistle to move and she began to whine and pull at the lead and scrabble with her paws at the base of the silver birch. He petted her and rubbed behind her ears and told her it was OK and he wouldn't be long. Then he walked back to the edge of the bank and eased himself over and slid down.

It was lying in the mud at his feet.

It had sunk down into the mud and he stooped and picked it out with the tips of his fingers and scraped off the thick globules of mud and wiped it on his coat. But he couldn't get the mud out from in between the keys and though he wiped as much off the screen as he could he could see that some of it had got under the screen and probably inside the phone as well and it was most likely ruined. He pressed some of the keys and nothing happened. The battery was probably dead too.

But at least it hadn't taken long to find it and he'd be back well before lunchtime. He heard Whistle yelping from the top of the bank and the sound of her paws scratching at the tree, and called out to her.

'OK, Whistle! Good girl! I'm coming now!'

Then he put the phone in his coat pocket and zipped the pocket, then turned to climb up the bank and he reached up and took hold of a root to pull himself up and the phone rang.

He let go of the root and dropped down. The phone was ringing in his pocket and he could feel it buzzing against his hip. He unzipped his pocket and took out the phone and looked at it. The screen light flashed on and off and it continued to ring but it didn't show any number. Just the screen flashing. And the buzzing. He pressed the answer pad and the ringing and the buzzing stopped and he put the phone against his ear.

There was a hiss and a harsh grating crackle, and a series of clicks, and the crackle again loud and sharp and rasping against his ear, and the hissing sound there all the time, sometimes loud sometimes soft, fading in and out, and they were noises of the deep and the dark, the underground cavern or the cold void. Then from far off there was a voice, and it was speaking and there were words, but he couldn't make them out, the voice was too far, too distant, and he heard it only for a moment before it was lost and all the sounds were lost beneath a single droning note that drummed against his ear and then shut off and there was silence.

He lowered the phone. It was dead.

It had been dead before but he'd heard those noises and he'd heard that voice. Someone calling to him. Trying to be heard.

He just wanted to get back.

He put the dead phone back in his pocket, zipped the pocket and took hold of the root, hauled himself up and clambered to the top of the bank.

The dog was gone.

The lead was still lashed around the trunk of the silver birch and the end with the clasp was still pushed through the hand loop, but it was lying flat on the ground and the dog's collar was lying there too, still attached. He could see where she'd clawed at the tree and at the earth around the tree and in all her frantic clawing and tugging at the lead she must have somehow slipped her neck out of the collar. But why hadn't she come down to him? Why had she run off? It must have happened while he was listening to the noises coming from the phone.

He took the lead and the collar from round the tree and then set off along the path around the pool calling her name. And he was trying hard not to think about what had happened the last time he'd lost her, and trying to keep the panic from knotting his stomach. He was trying his best to stay calm and just to find her, because she must be here somewhere and she can't have gone far, and so he made his way all around the pool and back to where he'd started from, and then he went along the other tracks and pathways that threaded and wound through the woods, calling her name and calling her name, but she didn't come and he didn't see her.

He stopped at last on the wooden bridge facing the pool and tried to think clearly. The dog wasn't here. If she was he'd have found her. So she must have left the woods. Gone back out into the field. Or up to the canal. He'd probably find her there waiting for him and wagging her tail.

He was wrong.

She wasn't in the field and she wasn't on the bridge. He stood in the middle and looked back the way they'd come and he couldn't see her there, then he looked over the other side where the canal ran past the Lime Pits and on towards the town and he couldn't see her there either. He stood with both hands gripping the top of the bridge. He felt its crumbling brickwork beneath his palms and fingers. Then he let go of the bridge and walked to the metal gate that opened into the field where the farm was. He climbed up and stood on one of the bars and looked out into the field towards the farm. Then he climbed down and stood on the bridge facing the wood. And all the time he was trying to keep it down, trying to stop it from rising up through him, with his fists clenched in front of him, gripping at the air as they'd gripped the bridge, holding on so that he wouldn't stumble and fall off the edge and drop down into it.

The darkness and the chaos down there.

The noises and the voices and black mist swirling.

He was going to hold on with his feet placed here firmly on the bridge and he was going to think what to do and he was going to find the dog.

And then he saw her.

She trotted out of the wood and stood on the track at the bottom of the field looking at him.

He unclenched his fists.

'Whistle!' he called. 'Come, girl! Come on! Whistle, come!'

She didn't move. She stood there looking up at him.

That was all right, though, it was fine, because he'd found her now and he'd just walk down there and he wouldn't be angry or shout at her, he'd walk down there and slip the collar back round her neck and make sure it was on tight and then take her back up to the canal and then back to his aunt's house.

But as he drew closer to her he sensed that there

was something wrong. Something about the way she just stood there looking at him. The way she was standing. Not like Whistle. Her body seeming to be stiff and her head pushed down and forward between her shoulder blades and her ears lying flat along her head.

He slowed his pace.

Her teeth were bared. And now he could hear her growling.

It was a low growl deep in her throat and as he approached it grew louder and rose to become a hard-edged rasping snarl that came out from between her bared teeth and it made him stop. He looked at her and what he saw in her face was savagery and rage and blood-thirst and as he spoke her name and began to back off she lunged forward and the snarl lifted its note again to a yowling scream as she lifted off the ground and sprang through the air and was flung towards him on the rising arc of that scream with her jaws wide to clamp and tear and bite through. And then as he stumbled back with his arms raised for protection she suddenly checked in mid-air as if dragged back by some invisible lead and her body twisted round and the growling scream was yanked back too and became a yelp and then she dropped suddenly to the ground and lay on her side, still, with an arrow in her neck.

He lowered his arms and stood looking at the dog. Then he walked up to where she lay. She was on her side, forelegs splayed out in front, teeth still bared. The arrow stuck up from her neck. She was completely still, not even a shudder of movement. And he did not take note then but he recalled it afterwards that there was no blood. He looked down at her for a while then raised his head and looked up and across to his right. At the edge of the field where a hedge ran down from the canal bank to the wood, he saw a figure.

It was standing by a gap in the hedge looking towards him, and as soon as he saw it he began to run across the field towards the figure. He was shouting, calling out, not words, just sounds coming from his mouth, yelling so his throat hurt, and his knees hurting as they jarred against the lumps of furrows, and the mud sucking at his trainers, dragging at him, so that suddenly his foot twisted, and he fell, hard and heavy, wrists and elbows jarred, face smarting where it scraped against stones and grit, and when he pushed himself up to his feet and looked the figure was gone.

He was close to tears, but holding them back, like he was holding everything else back, gripping tight and not letting go, and he turned and walked back across the field in the pale wet-looking light under the featureless sky to where the dog lay dead with the arrow in her neck. Only when he got there the dog was gone and there was just the arrow lying crossways on the track.

And then he couldn't hold any of it back any more, not the tears or anything.

Sixteen

Real

A door.

A door standing upright in the field. Across the track. Nothing around it. Just the door.

The attic door.

And it's closed.

Nothing for it. Open the door.

It swings open on darkness.

An immensity of darkness with no end to it. A darkness that just is, and is for ever. But is not silent. This darkness speaks.

Hisses and crackles, screechings and grindings and howlings, click and rasp and sputter and whine. And a voice calling.

Dark laughter.

There's someone there. Someone watching. Waiting in the darkness. Here I am, ready or not.

Coming to get you.

Dark laughter, close.

Now something is moving in the darkness. A black mist winding and twisting. A ribbon of smoke.

151

Thickening, coagulating. A jellied mass glistening. Name it, quick. Fix it. Frogspawn.

No. It's changing. And growing. A different form. Sucking all the darkness into that form. Neck unfolding, wings spreading. It rears up, monstrous. Turns its head. An eye looking. Your own image trapped in the black pupil.

The eye blinked.

A beak. Feathers.

A crow.

A crow in an empty field, looking at you.

Dull light, grey sky.

The muddy, furrowed earth. The bare branches of trees.

Your eyes looking at the crow that's looking at you.

Now and here. Real.

The crow hopped a few paces across the furrows. It stopped and lowered its back and pushed its neck and head forward and gave a long, dry-ratchet croak. Then it opened out its wings and flew off. Nathan watched it cross the field. A few other crows flew up and joined it and they made their way over towards the canal, keeping low.

He was the only living thing to be seen in the field now.

He bent down and picked up the arrow from the track. It had a shaft of dark-grained and shiny wood. At one end, notched and glued into the shaft, were four flights of feathers, brown, speckled with white. He ran his thumb along the edge of one of them and the barbs made a dry, bristling whisper and sprang back into shape when he lifted his thumb. At the other end was an oval-shaped stone, worked and chipped and shaped and polished, honed to a point, its edges razor sharp. Flint. It was pushed into a notch and tied fast with some kind of thread that was stiff to the touch and the thread had been painted over with some kind of brown glue. He laid the arrow across the palm of his hand, felt the balance of lightness and weight. He ran his finger along the shaft and felt the smoothness of the wood. He closed the fingers of his hand over it. He felt it solid in his hand.

This too was real.

He'd seen the dog struck by the arrow. He'd seen the dog fall and lie still with the arrow sticking up out of her neck.

And that had been real.

He'd seen a figure standing by the hedge and he'd run towards the figure and fallen and then the figure was gone.

And the dog was gone too but the arrow that

had struck the dog and stuck out of her neck was here. He held it in his hand.

Please, he thought. Let it all be real.

Then he set off along the track to the wood.

She was at the bottom of the bank snuffling along the water's edge near the place where he'd picked up his phone. He stood at the top of the bank. The dog hadn't seen him and he was nervous at first of calling her but then he did call her and she turned her head and saw him and came scrambling up the side of the bank and stood wagging her tail and pushing her nose forward into his hand. He rubbed her head and ears and scratched her throat and then unstrapped the collar and put it round her neck and strapped it again and made sure that the lead was secure. Then he sat on a root and she sat with her head between his knees and he stroked and fussed her some more.

The thing to do now was not to think about any of it or try to make sense of it but just to get her out of the wood and away from the Lime Pits. The thing was to get back onto the canal and then for the two of them to run all the way along the towpath to the road bridge and then climb up to the road and get back to his aunt and uncle's house. They could still be back by lunchtime. Before his aunt came home from her shift. Just get back there and then think about what had happened and try to make sense of it later. Because it was all connected, all of it, somehow, everything that happened. And if it was all real then it all meant something and it would all make sense when he'd worked it out. And he would work it out after he got back. So that's what he was going to do.

Then he heard a girl's voice behind him.

'Give me my arrow.'

She told him her name was Rasha and that she was hunting a creature which she called *terastos*. *Terastos* was not the creature's name, it was what the creature was, a thing to be feared. The creature itself had no name. It was the Creature. And as it had no name, neither did it have form or size, but could take on any shape it wished or that was wished upon it, and it dwelt in a place that was beyond all time and beyond all worlds; she called it *vatharos*, which he didn't understand. This Creature was the thing he had seen in the sky above the trees, and which had dropped down into the pool and it was there now, gathering its strength and growing in power. But it was not only there. It was in all things and in all times and all places.

They were sitting together on the bank above the water. He was crouched forward on the root and she was seated cross-legged on the cloak that she wore which she had taken off and spread on the ground. She wore a belt and there was a knife in it. Neither of them looked at each other. Both looked at the pool. Whistle was lying in between them and the lead was hanging loosely from Nathan's hand. He listened to what she told him, and he didn't think if he understood it or not, or if he believed in this Creature; he didn't wonder how it was she knew that he had seen it drop from the sky. Because she was sitting there with him, this strange girl in her strange clothes and her strange way of speaking, she was sitting there on the cloak or robe that seemed to be made of some kind of animal skin, and she was real, and the cloak was real, and the knife in her belt was real, and the belt, that was real too. And he wanted all that to be real, and he wanted what she was telling him to be real, too, because if it was real, it made sense. It meant something. So he listened, sitting there on the root with her sitting on the cloak and the dog lying between them and let her tell him about the Creature.

It was a creature from before the beginning of things, the time of chaos before creation took form and became fixed. It was a part of creation that had remained unfixed, and its desire was to return all things to chaos. To break the bonds that held things together. For all to become as it was.

'When people fight each other,' she said. 'When

the rules are broken. When no one remembers where they come from and what they are for. When there is anger and hatred and pain in the heart. These are the dreams of this Creature working in the world.'

The water appeared still but when you looked closely you saw that its surface was moving all the time, little strokes and shudders and stipples, glints and flickers. Tiny creatures stroking the skin of the water with their delicate feet. And there were rustlings in the reeds, and sometimes you glimpsed a coot or a moorhen there, and they were all living their lives.

Sometimes the Creature itself rose into the world. A voice would call it. A voice crying out in anger or hatred or pain. Sometimes the voice would not know it was calling the Creature, but it called all the same. Then the Creature woke and came into the world; it fed on that anger and hatred and pain until it grew strong. Then it took form and shape in the world. Then it made itself known. Then it was a *terastos*, a creature to be feared. And to be fought and destroyed.

Though he did not know the word, *terastos*, he thought he knew what it meant.

'This is why I am here,' she said. 'Why I have come to this world. To fight the Creature. To overcome it, send it back to its *vatharos.'*

It was the Old Woman who had told her she must seek the Creature. The Old Woman was training her to be a *yiera*. This was another word he didn't understand and he couldn't guess at its meaning. The Old Woman had been the *yiera* for the people for many years, but now she was growing near to the time for her passing, and a new *yiera* must be found to dream for the people. The Old Woman had found her, and it was the Old Woman who had told her all these things she was telling him now, and that too was part of the duty of a *yiera*, to be a keeper of the stories and memories of the people. In this way the people knew who they were and where they had come from and what they were for. The Creature was the enemy of this. To become a *yiera* she must prove herself strong. She must seek out some enemy and face it alone. And it must be her spirit self that did this. Her spirit must go out from her body into the spirit world and there in the spirit world she would find the enemy and overpower it. Then she would return to the real world and her body would wake and the people would be safe and she would be a true *yiera*, the dreamer and lawkeeper and protector of the people.

The rope hung down from the branch over the pool. Beyond the rope there was the island and there was a heron on the island. It stood close to the water's edge with its neck hunched into its shoulders and was completely still. Its yellow eyes were fixed with intent on the water. It was watching, hunting. Close to the bank above where they sat there was a splash and ripples from the splash spread out over the surface of the water. They lapped gently against the shore of the island. The heron remained still.

She continued speaking to him of the Creature, telling him how it lay at the bottom of the pool, growing in strength and drawing on the anger and the fear of the one who had called it to bring it that strength. And he only stopped her once to ask her a question that suddenly came to him, and that was if she came from some other world or time or place how was it she spoke his language. And she said she didn't know what he meant, she was speaking her own language and so was he. Then he didn't say anything else and carried on listening as she spoke and told him more.

'It is still not strong enough to rise,' she said. 'But soon it will be. It grows stronger. It has darkness to feed it and it has found shapes it can wear to try its power in the world.'

Something was swimming across the pool from the bank towards the island. A rippled *V* spread out from its nose where it pushed through the water. It was a rat.

The dog had been one of the shapes the Creature had taken. It had taken the form of the dog not from the dog itself but from the picture of the dog that he held in his mind and in that form it had shown itself to him to demonstrate its growing power. Her arrow had broken that power, but only for a time. Its dragging of the other boy under the water had too been a demonstration of its power.

The dog was not the only form it had taken. There was another that came from the deepest fear and anger of the one who had called it.

The rat had reached the island but it had not seen the heron. It was a young rat, not fully grown, and as it crawled out onto the shore, in a single smooth and pure movement the heron arched its neck and stabbed forward and down and speared the rat on its beak. Then still with the same graceful arc of movement it spread its wings and lifted up off the island and away across the tops of the trees with the rat struggling on the point of its beak and all the time screaming. The screams continued for a little while after the heron could no longer be seen. Then they stopped.

He turned and looked at the girl. She had been watching what had happened with the rat and the heron as well and her eyes were still looking towards where the heron had flown over the trees.

She was small and dark-haired and her skin was dark too. She wasn't old, about the same age as his cousin, but there was something about her that made her seem much older. Not like a child. Not like anyone he knew. He remembered that she had told him her name was Rasha, and her strangeness and the strangeness of it all overwhelmed him for a moment and he began to tremble and there was the buzzing in his head and the dark mist began to form. But he held on to the reality of being there on the bank with this girl and of the dog lying between them and himself sitting on the root of the tree, and he asked her how she knew he had seen the Creature and about Joe being dragged under the water.

She looked at him then and from a small pouch that hung at her belt beside the knife she took out a thin disc made of some dark, polished stone.

'This showed me,' she said.

He asked her what it was and she told him it was a mirror that showed things that had happened, or that may happen, or that were happening in other places.

'Things hidden from the eye,' she said.

She asked him if he wanted to look into it and he said yes.

Then Rasha held up the disc and he looked into it.

* * *

The girl lies on the wooden platform at the top of a tree. Her eyes are open but she does not move. It is night and the sky is clear and the moon is full and the light of the full moon illuminates her prone and seemingly lifeless body.

A circle of wooden torches are planted at the bottom of the tree and their lit flames gutter and flicker in darkness, and within this circle an Old Woman sits. She is wrapped in a cloak of bear skin and her eyes too are open and unblinking. Firelight from the torches plays across her ancient face, darkened and deeply scoured, and she is the only human present here though not the only figure.

Squatting also in the circle is a massive bear. Its coat is dark and shaggy, its forepaws rest on its haunches. Like a king cast out of his kingdom, though he carries that kingdom within him.

Its eyes glitter with a deep light, and that same light glitters in the Old Woman's eyes, and within each of those glittering pools of light a face is reflected. His face.

Looking back at himself out of the Old Woman's eyes and the eyes of the bear.

A star is falling from the sky. A star burning in the bright daylight, cutting a shimmering path through the air.

It touches a branch, and the branch bursts into flame. The flame dances on the branch-tip but does not consume it.

And the flame becomes a figure, the figure of a girl, a bow in her hand, her body shining.

The girl turns her head and looks at him.

Now there's darkness. And another figure in that darkness.

It stands, a shadow wrapped in shadow.

It is taking form out of the darkness.

The darkness coagulates about it. Stiffens. Thickens. Solidifies.

A scarecrow figure of rags and tatters. But living. And moving.

It eases free of the darkness. It takes a step. And a step. A step. And a step.

Slowly, surely, it advances.

It has no face.

* * *

She took the disc away and put it back in the pouch that hung from her belt. He looked at her.

'This is real.'

'Yes.'

'All of it. Real.'

'All of it.'

'You. And this thing. This monster. And what's been happening. Everything. It's real.'

'Yes.'

'Good. Because sometimes I've thought I've been going mad.'

So it was this Creature. This *terastos*, or monster. It didn't matter what it was. What mattered was that it was real. And it was real. He'd seen it in the sky. He'd seen it drop down into the pool. It was there now. It was real, and it was to blame for everything. The cold fingers grabbing at his foot, the eyes watching from the dark water. The smoke in his head, the buzzing, the tingling, the noises in the attic, the bad dreams, the blackouts. And Joe being dragged under, and the rat, and Kevin. And maybe his dad too. Maybe that. Everything that had happened, all the bad things, it was the Creature's fault, the Creature was to blame. It wasn't him. He wasn't to blame. So that was all right. He didn't have to worry about it any more. There was something else to blame and that was all right.

* * *

He was sitting looking across the pool. The girl sat nearby on the ground. The dog lay between them. The water shivered and rippled. Somewhere the heron was eating its kill. The girl was looking across the pool as well. But she wasn't seeing what he was seeing.

'So you're going to get rid of it.'

'Yes.'

'Send it back where it came from.'

'*Vatharos.*'

'Wherever. You'll send it back there.'

'Yes.'

'You're sure.'

'Yes.'

'You can beat this thing.'

'I must.'

'With that bow and those arrows.'

'They are my weapons.'

'What if you don't?'

'I will.'

'And everything will be all right, then.'

'Yes.'

He stood up. 'Right, then.' She turned her head and looked at him. 'I'll leave you to it.' He picked up the end of the lead. The dog stood and shook herself. The girl was staring at him. 'I'm going. Back home. To my uncle's house. Where I'm staying. I'm going back there now.' The girl said nothing but she just kept looking at him, staring hard. 'You don't need me. I'm no good at fighting. Ask anybody.' Her dark eyes fixed on his face. 'I'll see you. No, I won't. I'm not coming back here. This place. I'm done with it.' He gave a tug on the lead, then he and the dog began to walk towards the path, and once he was on the path he'd keep going, and not look back, just keep going along the path until he was out, and away, and gone, and be done with it all for good. And that was when the girl spoke to him.

'But it's not done with you. The Creature woke because it was called. I said this. It came here because a voice called it. It was your voice. It was you that called it.'

Seventeen

The Creature

First it broke through into light and air, following the one who had called it. And it was shapeless until the eyes saw it and began to give it form. There were wings and a body that twisted and writhed, and in this form it fell into the water.

It knew this form of old, and in the water's deep it began to figure and shape it. But it needed more. It needed to draw strength from the one who had called. To find the source of that voice, to tap into it and root itself there. It reached out and upwards, seeking. It sensed fear and reached out for that fear, and grabbed, and took hold. Fear became terror, and the terror gave it strength and it burrowed in.

Now it had somewhere to play, and there were things hidden here which it found out and examined. Different kinds of images and shapes, sounds and voices, things without a face or name. It tried them on and moved around in them, and each time it did this, the fear in the source grew stronger, and it fed on the fear and grew stronger itself. And there was one shape in particular that was strong in power.

At first it was like the others, a vague, nameless figure. But when it put this on there was a surge of energy, and not only fear, but rage too, and pain, and loss. And the more it moved around in this shape, the clearer it became. It found a voice for this figure, and it tried out the voice, and the voice worked. It found a name, and the name seemed to fit. And last of all it found a face. And all that energy and power, all that fear and rage and pain and loss were fixed in this face and concentrated there.

It put the face on.

Wearing that face, it grinned.

The other form, the one with wings and coiled neck and scales, still lay at the bottom of the pool. That would be useful later. But for now, this form, with this face, was the one it needed. Wearing this it would walk out into the world. Then cast it off like a dead skin, unfold its wings, and rise to power in all its majesty and terror.

For now it crouched among the spiders and the dust and the cobwebs. It muttered to itself, it chewed its broken teeth. It was the rag-man, the bone-man, the goblin in the attic. Bony fingers and ragged lips.

Waiting for the door to open.

Waiting for someone to come and find it.

Eighteen

Fall

His aunt wasn't back yet and his grandad was still asleep. He sat the dog on the floor in the kitchen and wiped her fur with the towel that was kept by her basket. Most of the mud came off her paws and underside, and after he'd let her off the lead he shook the towel outside and put it back in the basket. Then he half-filled the dog's bowl with dry food and filled her water bowl and put the bowls on the floor and while she was eating he took off his shoes and went upstairs to his room.

He took off his jeans because they were dirty and put on a clean pair. He folded his dirty jeans and put them in his suitcase with his other clothes. Then went to the bathroom and washed the mud off his hands and face, and swilled the sink clean. All the time he was doing this he was listening for his aunt to come back in from work but she didn't. Perhaps she'd decided to go shopping. He realized that he was hungry so he went back down to the kitchen to make himself a sandwich. Whistle had finished her food and drunk about half a bowl of water and now she was lying curled in her basket. She lifted her head and looked at him as he came in then lowered it again and closed her eyes.

There was no sound from the living room so before Nathan started making his sandwich he went in there to see if his grandad was awake yet and if he wanted a sandwich as well.

But his grandad was still asleep in his chair, and Nathan thought it was strange because he usually only took a nap for about twenty minutes. He'd been away a lot longer than that. Then he thought that there was something odd too about the way he was sitting in the chair. His body seemed more slumped than usual, more heavy-looking, and his head looked heavy too, the way it was hanging down and forward over his chest. Nathan walked up to his grandad. He was breathing, but it was coming fast and shallow and uneven. As if he was panting for breath. As if at any moment he might suddenly stop breathing.

'Grandad,' he said.

His grandad didn't move or wake. He just carried on sitting like that and breathing like that. His eyelids were flickering.

Nathan put his hand on his grandad's arm and shook him, and his grandad gave a sharp gasp and jerked his head up and stared at Nathan as if he didn't know where he was or who Nathan was.

'Grandad?' said Nathan. 'It's me.'

His grandad carried on staring at him, then he turned his head and stared at the room. He was still breathing quickly.

'Grandad,' said Nathan again. 'Are you all right?'

His grandad stared at him again.

'Don't go in there,' he said.

'What?'

'What?'

'You said—'

'Nathan,' said his grandad.

'Yes,' said Nathan.

'I've been asleep.'

'I know.'

'I was having a dream,' said his grandad. 'It was . . . ' His voice faltered and he stopped. Then he shook his head and eased himself up stiffly in the chair.

'How long have I been asleep?'

'A long time,' said Nathan. 'Over an hour.'

'You shouldn't have let me,' said his grandad.

'I didn't know,' said Nathan. 'I took Whistle out for a walk. I've only just come back.'

A puzzled look came over his grandad's face as if he was trying to remember something. Then it was gone and he grasped the arms of the chair with his

171

hands and tried to push himself up but he fell back again heavily.

'I feel a bit woozy,' he said. 'A bit giddy. Like I've been drinking.' He gave Nathan a look. 'I haven't been drinking.'

'I know,' said Nathan. He tried to think what to say. Then he said, 'I was just making a sandwich. Do you want one?'

'A sandwich? No. I could do with a cup of tea, though. Ask Theresa to make me a cup of tea.'

'She's not back from work,' said Nathan. 'I'll make you one.'

'All right,' said his grandad. Then he said, 'That dream I was having . . . ' But he stopped again. 'No good,' he said. 'It's gone. Perhaps it'll come back when I've had that tea.' He looked at Nathan again. 'Let it stand for five minutes before you pour it,' he said.

'I will,' said Nathan.

'And warm the pot before you put the teabag in.'

'Yes,' said Nathan, and he went into the kitchen to make the tea.

While he was making the tea his aunt came back from work. She asked if he'd had lunch yet and he told her he was going to make himself a sandwich and she said she'd make one for him and for herself and for his grandad. She asked him if Kevin was in and he told her he wasn't. Then he poured the tea into a mug and added milk and sugar and took it in to his grandad. His grandad's hand was trembling as he lifted the mug and he spilled some of the tea down his jumper but didn't seem to notice. He held the mug in front of his mouth with both hands, sipping at it and staring ahead over the top of the mug. Then a look came into his eyes as if he was remembering something and he spoke to Nathan.

'Do you still hear those noises from the attic?'

'Yes,' said Nathan. 'But I don't take any notice of them now.'

'Good,' said his grandad. 'Good. That's right. Yes. Don't take any notice.' He took a few more noisy sips of his tea. 'I wouldn't go in there, either,' he said. He sipped his tea. 'There's nothing there. You saw, didn't you? Just a lot of old junk.'

'Yes,' said Nathan.

'Yes,' said his grandad. 'That's all there is. So I wouldn't go in.'

He was going to ask his grandad why he'd said he shouldn't go in. He thought it was something to do with the dream he'd had. But he didn't have a chance because his aunt came in from the kitchen then and said that their sandwiches were ready.

He took the mug of tea from his grandad while he pushed himself up out of the chair and carried it as they both went through into the kitchen. His aunt had made cheese and salad sandwiches and set them on plates and the three of them sat down to eat them together. His grandad drank his tea and nibbled at one of his sandwiches, and his aunt asked why he wasn't eating and he said he wasn't hungry. He said he might have them later. He said again that he was feeling a bit woozy, a bit wobbly, and thought he might be coming down with a cold, or something, so his aunt gave him a couple of paracetamol which he took with his tea, and she said perhaps he ought to go upstairs and have a lie down and he said he thought he would. He asked Nathan if he'd go with him up the stairs, just in case he fell down them, and the way he said it he tried to make it sound like a joke but Nathan could tell that underneath the joke he was serious. Nathan had finished his sandwich and his grandad drank up his tea, and then they both stood and Nathan followed his grandad out of the kitchen and into the hall. As they were going out his aunt asked him if he knew where Kevin had gone and when he'd be back and he answered no to both questions.

'I think I'll give his room a clean and tidy,' she said. 'It hasn't been done for a week and it'll be in a right state.'

She wasn't saying this to Nathan or his grandad,

just to herself, so Nathan didn't say anything back and he and his grandad went into the hall.

His grandad walked slowly and heavily up the stairs and Nathan walked behind him, watching how he gripped the banister with his hand and pulled himself up from one step to the next.

'I don't know what's the matter with me today,' he said. 'Getting old, I suppose.'

'You're not old,' said Nathan.

'I feel it today.'

'Perhaps it's that dream you had, Grandad,' said Nathan.

They were at the top of the stairs now outside the door to his grandad's bedroom, and his grandad was standing with his hands resting on the rail that ran along the landing.

'A dream,' said his grandad.

'You said you had a dream.'

'A dream. I did. Yes.' His grandad had that puzzled, trying-to-remember-something look in his eyes again. 'I did have a dream. You woke me out of it. Some dreams can leave you feeling funny,' he said.

Then Nathan said, 'I wondered if it might have been about the attic.'

'Why?'

'Because you said about not going in there.'

His grandad looked hard at Nathan.

'Yes,' he said, 'I did.' Then he gave a short, breathy laugh. 'But I can't remember why.'

Then he said thank you to Nathan for coming up the stairs with him and went into his room. And Nathan went into his own room.

He was lying on the bed going over what the girl Rasha had said to him, trying to remember her words, to sort them and arrange them so that they made sense, trying to get the whole thing clear in his head.

The Creature fed on pain and fear. It used them to grow stronger. It was feeding on something in him. The same thing that had called to it. He hadn't known he'd called to it. It was the thing inside him that had called. Something that kept itself hidden away in the dark. Something that wanted to come into the light. Like the Creature. That's why it called to the Creature. It thought the Creature would help it and the Creature pretended that it would help but it wouldn't. The Creature would use the something inside him to bring itself into the light and then throw the something off, and leave it empty and useless and dead. And him too. Because the something that had called was a part of him. It was the fear and anger and pain part of him, and the Creature was taking its form and

176

shape from it. It needed a shape to come into the world. A living form. And the form it was taking would be one that he knew. It would speak to him. He would recognize it. But he must not let it deceive him. He must stand firm, resist it. If he did that it would not be able to come fully into its power, and then she would be able to fight it, and defeat it.

But first he must face it. And he realized what that meant. He would have to go into the attic.

The girl had seemed to know all about that. About all that had been happening. About the attic.

But he'd thought the Creature was in the pool, he'd said to her. He'd seen it come down into the pool. She'd told him it was in the pool. It couldn't be in the pool and in the attic, he'd said.

She'd told him it could. It could be in the pool and in the attic and in any place and in any thing and in any person it chose. In any shape it chose. And it had chosen two shapes. The one in the pool was for her. The one in the attic was for him. He must face it and defeat it in the attic and she must face it and defeat it in the pool.

He must go into the attic.

But he didn't want to go into the attic. He didn't want to fight this creature. That's why she was here. Why should he have to fight this creature as well?

Because it was going to destroy him. Him and

those around him. It was already working on them. Causing rift. Bringing conflict. And it would work on them like this until it destroyed all of them. And then it would come into the world and do the same.

So he would have to go into the attic.

But she could see he was scared. She knew it was a hard thing for him to do. So she would give him something. A thing that had power. He could use it to protect himself. It would help him to resist the Creature and defeat it.

When he went into the attic.

She had given it to him and then he had come back and now he lay on his bed going over what she had said to him, remembering her words, getting the whole thing straight and clear in his head.

He sat up and reached over to where his jacket hung on the chair and put his hand in the near-side pocket and took out the disc the girl had given him. She had said that it was made from a rare and precious kind of stone that had been chipped and worked into this form, and polished smooth so that you could see things in it. Sometimes it reflected only what was shown to it. Sometimes it showed things that could not be seen with the eye. It had a power and the power would help him. He sat on the edge of the bed with the disc in his hand and his hand resting on his knee and looking straight ahead. Then he lifted the disc and lowered his head and looked into it.

All he saw was his own face looking back.

Then his mobile beeped.

It was the sound it made when there was a message. He sat and listened as it beeped again. He knew it couldn't beep. He knew there couldn't be a message. His phone was dead. He knew that.

It had been dead when he'd found it at the pool. When he'd heard the hissing crackling noises and the voice from far off.

It beeped. There was a message.

He laid the disc on the bed and stood up in front of the chair and reached into his jacket pocket and took out the phone. It beeped. The screenlight flashed. He looked at the words on the screen.

'New message.'

He pressed the key. He read the words.

'Receiving message.'

The words went off the screen. The message screen came up. It was blank.

He stared at the blank screen.

Then with his other hand he picked up the disc from the bed and held it at an angle to the phone so that he could see the phone reflected in the surface of the disc. He looked at the reflection of the screen in the disc. There was a message on the screen. The letters of the message were back to front but he could tell what they said. Even so, to be certain, he put the phone and the disc down and took his notebook and pen from his backpack and looked at the reflected message in the disc again and wrote down the message and then wrote it out underneath the right way round. He sat looking at the words he'd written on the paper.

'I'm here. I'm waiting. Come and find me.'

He looked at them and read them and then he closed his book. Then he looked at his phone. The screen was blank and the phone was dead.

Don't go in there.

He stood at the bottom of the three stairs that led up to the attic.

I wouldn't go in there.

He was looking up at the attic door.

Don't go in. That's what his grandad had said. *I wouldn't go in there.*

But you're not me, Grandad.

He put his hand in his pocket and felt the disc there. He kept his hand on the disc. Then took a step towards the stairs.

But then he heard the door at the end of the landing open and he turned and saw his aunt coming through the doorway towards him and she was holding something in her hand.

'Nathan. Do you know anything about this?'

It was Kevin's air-pistol. She held it up in front of her and stood in front of him talking at him.

'Have you seen it before? I just found it in his room. Did you know Kevin had it? Nathan? I'm asking you.'

He was staring at the air-pistol in her hand. He tried to shake his head but it just came as a kind of twitching movement that he hoped would look as if he was saying no but didn't mean anything, which meant he wouldn't have lied. But his aunt wasn't going to let it go at that.

'Nathan,' she said, 'I'm waiting for an answer. Did you know about this?'

She stood there waiting for his answer.

'Yes,' he said.

'When did you see it? Yesterday? When you went over the Lime Pits? Did he take it with him?'

Somehow she seemed to know the answers already. But she had to hear them from him.

'Yes,' he said again.

'Did he fire it?'

'No.'

'Are you sure?'

'He didn't fire it, Aunt Theresa.'

'And I suppose he told you not to say anything about it.'

'Yes.'

'He would. He knew what would happen if we

found out about it. And now I have. And he's going to hear what I have to say about it.'

She turned and walked back along the landing and through the door and closed it firmly behind her. Nathan looked at the closed door then turned around and looked up at the attic door.

I'm here. I'm waiting. Come and find me.

Then he went back to his own room.

They were in the kitchen having tea when Kevin came in and said he didn't want anything to eat because he'd had something at his friend's house, but Nathan's aunt said she wanted him to sit with them, so he got himself a can from the fridge and sat and tore off the ring-pull and took a drink from the can.

'I wish you'd drink that from a glass,' said Nathan's uncle.

'I'm saving washing-up,' said Kevin.

'Get yourself a glass,' said Nathan's aunt. She wasn't looking at Kevin when she said it and there was a hard edge to her voice, a brittle note of warning, and Kevin stood up and went to the wall-cupboard and opened it and took out a glass, then closed the cupboard door and sat and poured the drink from the can into the glass.

No one said anything for a few minutes. They'd

been eating grilled chicken with chips and peas and grilled tomatoes and Nathan had almost finished. There was only one grilled tomato left and he didn't want it but he was making himself eat it because it was better than putting down his knife and fork and perhaps having to look at Kevin. He didn't want to look at Kevin, and he looked at the grilled tomato on his plate and watched himself cut it into pieces and watched the cooked juices and the seeds run out onto the plate.

His aunt and uncle were looking at the remainder of the food on their plates as well.

'Where's Grandad?' said Kevin.

'He's not feeling very well,' said Nathan's uncle.

'Oh,' said Kevin, and he took another drink from his glass. Then he said, 'Can I go and play a game on the computer?'

'Stay here,' said Nathan's aunt.

'What for?' said Kevin. 'What do you want?'

'Just sit down till we've finished.'

Kevin sat and Nathan ate the last of his tomato and put his knife and fork on his plate. He glanced up quickly at Kevin. Kevin had both hands cupped around his glass and was staring at the glass and he knew now that something was wrong and was waiting to find out what it was so that it could start happening, and Nathan knew what it was and was waiting for it to happen as well, and he was getting that tingling in his fingers and the humming sound far off in the back of his head.

His aunt and uncle finished eating and his aunt collected up the plates and the knives and the forks and took them to the work surface next to the sink and stacked them there ready for washing up. Still nobody said anything and Nathan could feel the humming growing louder into the buzzing noise and the tingling in his fingers was starting to spread up through his hands. When his aunt came back she had the air-pistol and she put it down in the middle of the table. It made a hard sound as she put it down and Kevin stared at the air-pistol lying on the table and still nobody said anything.

Then his aunt Theresa spoke.

'Where did this come from?' she said.

Kevin didn't answer. He just carried on staring at the air-pistol and Nathan saw his face go red, the redness rising up from his neck in blotches to spread across his ears and his cheeks and around his eyes.

'Kevin,' said his uncle Rob. 'Answer your mother.'

But he didn't say anything to Nathan's aunt or uncle. Instead he looked across the table at Nathan, and Nathan saw that there was a redness in his eyes as well, a rage and a fury, and Nathan felt the tingling running through his wrists into his arms, and heard the buzzing loud in his head.

'Did you tell them?' said Kevin.

'No,' said Nathan.

'You did,' said Kevin. 'You little prat, you told them!'

'Kevin!' His aunt's voice was loud and sharp, a slap in the air. 'This is nothing to do with Nathan. It's to do with you! Now I'm asking you again, where did you get it?'

Kevin looked away from Nathan and stared at his hands. He'd taken them from the glass and they were resting on the table on either side of the glass with their palms down. He spoke keeping his eyes fixed on his hands.

'How'd you find it then if he didn't tell you?'

'It doesn't matter how your mother found it,' said Uncle Rob. 'That's not the point. The point is she did find it.'

'She was snooping.'

'Kevin!'

'I was cleaning your room.'

'Snooping.'

'That's enough!'

'She couldn't have found it if she hadn't been snooping.'

'Because you had it hidden away.'

Kevin didn't say anything. The buzzing was loud.

'Because you didn't want us to know you had it.'

He didn't say anything. The tingling was running up his arms, it was in his neck.

'Because we told you before you couldn't have one so you went out and got one behind our backs.'

Kevin stared at his hands. They were flat on the table on either side of the glass. It was happening inside him with the buzzing and the black mist and the tingling. His face was red and blotchy and he was staring at his hands. The buzzing and the black mist and the tingling were joining together to make something happen and first it was happening inside him but then it would happen outside. Kevin stared at his hands that were on the table on either side of the glass.

'So I'm going to ask you again,' said Aunt Theresa. 'Where did you get it?'

Now Kevin spoke but he kept looking at his hands.

'None of your business.'

'What?'

'None of your business.'

'Say that again. Go on, Kevin.'

'Theresa.'

'I want to hear him say it again. Kevin! Say it again!'

Kevin's hands were still on the table but now the wrists were bending up and the fingers were spreading and the hands were pressing down and

Kevin was standing up and as he was standing up the chair he'd been sitting on fell backwards and clattered against the kitchen dresser, and he was leaning forwards over his hands, pushing his face at Aunt Theresa and it was red and blotchy and he was shouting.

'It's none of your business where I got it cos it's mine, I paid for it with my paper-round money and you ain't taking it off me!'

His words came out in a rush and a kind of cracked and high-pitched scream so that you almost didn't hear the words; it wasn't the words that were important, it was the voice with its scream, its howl of anger and rage and fury. Nathan saw his aunt flinch back from the scream and he knew that this was it, it was happening now, because the buzzing and the tingling and the black mist were gone, there was only the sound of Kevin's voice and what was happening was happening there now. His aunt flinched from it, he saw her, he saw her draw back from the fury of the voice. And the table seemed to flinch too, it shook, or stumbled, as Kevin leaned and pressed into it, pushing down with his hands as he pushed out with his red blotchy face and his screaming voice, and Nathan saw the glass between his hands shake and then tumble forwards, and he saw the dark liquid spilling out and spreading over the table, and it was like the darkness that had been inside his head, growing and spreading, but now it was out there on the table, everything was out there.

Nathan's uncle was standing up. He didn't remember him standing but there he was now, standing up, and there was Kevin standing leaning over the table and his aunt standing back from Kevin and the scream of rage, of anger and fury that seemed to be going on long after the words had finished. It was all he could hear and he watched everything happen through the scream. He watched his uncle reach out with both his hands and grab Kevin by the shoulders and turn him round to face him. He watched Kevin pull his arms back and up and take hold of Uncle Rob's hands and push them away from him and he saw Uncle Rob stumble backwards and he saw too the look of shock and surprise on his uncle's face. And he was still looking at that and seeing everything through the scream when he became aware of another movement and he turned and saw Kevin swinging round to face Aunt Theresa again and his face was red and his mouth was open, but it was Aunt Theresa who was pulling him round to face her with one hand, and the other hand was coming round through the air, coming right round from behind Aunt Theresa's head, open with its fingers closed together, and it came round fast and sharp onto the side of Kevin's face and there was a loud crack and the screaming stopped.

Then there was this silence. And everything was very still inside the silence. Kevin stared at Aunt Theresa and the side of his face where she'd slapped him was a brighter red than the rest of his face, and this redness was in the shape of his aunt's fingers. And as Kevin stared at her she was staring, no, glaring, at him, and the rage and the anger and the fury that had been in Kevin's voice seemed to be in her eyes now. And though Nathan couldn't see him he could feel his uncle standing to his side and a little behind him. And everybody was looking and they were all inside the stillness and the complete silence.

Then there was the sound of something falling heavily upstairs.

Nathan came to the top of the stairs behind his aunt and uncle. They were on the landing kneeling down and in between them was his grandad lying twisted half on his side and half on his back at the bottom of the attic stairs.

Nineteen

Got You

The X-ray showed that he had fractured his hip in the fall and this would mean having to have an operation to repair it. The surgeon would probably be able to operate the next day although it might have to be the day after and then he would need to stay in hospital for some time after that until he was able to move around again without too much pain. They couldn't say exactly how long. It would depend on how quickly he recovered. But he seemed to be generally fit and healthy and they didn't think it would take too long. Of course there would need to be someone at home with him once he did leave the hospital.

Nathan's aunt and uncle had taken his grandad to hospital after the accident and Nathan had gone with them. Kevin hadn't. By the time his grandad had been seen by a doctor in Accident and Emergency and had had his X-ray done and been admitted to a ward and settled, it was late night and Nathan was falling asleep in the back of the car as they drove home. He lay curled up on the seat and the voices of his aunt and uncle as they spoke to each other wove in and out of the drone of the engine and the hiss and grumble of the wheels and the rhythmic click and swish of the wipers on the windscreen because while they'd been all that time in the hospital it had started to rain.

They were speaking about Grandad and his aunt was saying that it would mean his aunt having to take time off work to look after him when he came out, and she hoped they wouldn't mind, it might mean having to make it part of her holiday, and it was a real nuisance. Then he lost their voices for a time because suddenly the girl was there and he was by the pool and she was telling him how it wasn't done with him because he was the one who'd called it and he had got to go in there, then his grandad was telling him not to go in there because he was getting old, and then his grandad spoke to him again but it wasn't his grandad's voice and he was saying come and find me. Then their voices came back again and they were wondering what he was doing up there anyway, especially when he wasn't feeling well, and Kevin screamed and said none of your business and his aunt said say that again but he didn't, instead he said to Nathan it was you who told them, you're the one that called it. Then his uncle was wondering what he was looking for in there and the girl told him it was things hidden from the eye, *vatharos*, she said over and over again, *vatharos vatharos vatharos* and her voice was a hiss, like the hiss of the wheels and the swish of the wipers, *vatharos vatharos,* and then it was just the hum and drone of the engine and somebody saying they were coming to get him.

It was late when he woke the next morning. His aunt had left a letter for him on the kitchen table saying that she'd gone to work and that after work she was going straight to the hospital to visit Grandad and take him some things that he needed. She wouldn't be back until about half-past four. There was plenty to eat for breakfast and for lunch and he was not to go out anywhere but stay at home. She also wrote that she'd phoned his mum and told her what had happened and that his mum was getting the train back today. She'd probably arrive some time in the afternoon, or by evening at the latest.

He put the letter back on the table and made himself some toast and poured some milk into a glass and sat eating the toast and drinking the milk and reading again the letter from his aunt. He thought about his mother coming back, and about the girl at the Lime Pits, Rasha her name was, and what she'd told him, and Grandad going into the attic and falling down the stairs, or did something push him? The row between his aunt and uncle and Kevin, as well, just before his grandad fell, that seemed to be part of everything that was happening, not separate from it, part of things falling apart that the girl had talked about, what it was the Creature lived on and fed on, what it made happen. And he wanted his mother's coming back to make a difference to it all, to make everything all right again, because that was how it was supposed to be when your mother came back. But he knew as he bit into his toast and drank his milk that it wasn't like that any more, her coming back didn't make any difference, and this Creature or whatever it was that was in the attic was still in there waiting for him to go up there and find it.

Well, if it was waiting for him it could wait. He wasn't ready yet.

He stood up and took two more slices of bread from the bread bin and put them in the toaster and then filled the kettle and plugged it back in and switched it on to make himself a cup of tea and the hallway door opened and Kevin came in.

'How's Grandad?' said Kevin.

'He fractured his hip,' said Nathan. 'He's got to have an operation.'

Kevin stood in the kitchen. He didn't sit down.

'Do you want some toast and some tea?' said Nathan.

Kevin shook his head. He went to the fridge and opened it and took out a can and pulled off the ring pull and took a long swig from the can.

'I didn't tell,' said Nathan. 'She found it. She was cleaning your room. I was going to warn you when you came back but you didn't come back.'

'You could've phoned my mobile.'

'My phone's dead. And I don't know your number.'

Kevin shrugged.

'It don't matter anyway. They can't make me get rid of it.'

He took another drink from the can, then he said, 'I've got something to show you.'

'What?' said Nathan.

'Something I found,' said Kevin.

'What is it?'

'It's upstairs.'

'What is it, though?'

'A surprise. Come on.'

He put his can on the table.

'I'm making some tea.'

'The kettle hasn't boiled yet. It won't take long.'

'Why don't you tell me what it is you've found?'

'Cos it's a surprise and I want to show you.'

Kevin was walking out of the kitchen into the hall. He left the door open. Nathan watched him walk down the hall to the bottom of the stairs. Kevin stopped there and turned to look at Nathan.

'Come on. It's to do with why Grandad was in the attic.'

Nathan followed him into the hall. Kevin began to climb the stairs.

'Did you go in there?' said Nathan. 'Did you find something in there?'

'You'll see in a minute.'

Kevin was at the top of the stairs now and going towards the attic stairs.

'Tell me.'

Kevin stood at the bottom of the three stairs and waited for Nathan.

'It's better to show you,' he said.

Nathan stood looking up at the attic door. Kevin stood beside him.

'There's nothing in there,' said Nathan. 'I've looked.'

'You haven't looked hard enough,' said Kevin.

'It's just boxes and furniture.'

'Don't forget the bogeyman.' Kevin tried to make his voice sound scary. 'The bogeyman,' he said, 'moving around in the middle of the night.'

'There's no such thing,' said Nathan.

'That's what you think,' said Kevin, and he

grabbed hold of Nathan's arms. 'Got you now, you little sneak.' And started to drag him up the stairs towards the door.

'What you doing, Kevin?' Nathan shouted. 'Get off!'

He was struggling to pull himself free but Kevin was bigger than he was, and stronger, and his fingers were gripped tight round Nathan's arms, squeezing into them, hard, hurting, so that he squealed in pain, and Kevin laughed as he pulled him onto the top step. Still he tried to twist himself free, and kicked against the stairs and the stair-rail and the door and Kevin's legs, but then Kevin let go one of his arms and put his hand around his throat and shoved him up against the door so that the back of his head banged against it, and Kevin held him there, pushing his face up close to his.

'You told,' he said. 'You told about my air-pistol.'

'No, I didn't,' said Nathan.

'Yes, you did,' said Kevin. 'I know you did. And now you're going to pay.'

'What you mean?'

'Scared of the attic, ain't you? Scared of the bogeyman in the attic.'

'No, I'm not.' He was finding it hard to talk because of Kevin's hand pushed up under his chin and his fingers squeezing his throat. 'I'm not scared of anything in there cos there's nothing.'

196

'So what was Grandad looking for?' He was grinning close up to Nathan's face. 'What did he find? What was it pushed him down the stairs?'

'I don't know,' said Nathan.

'Well, you're going to find out,' said Kevin, and he pulled Nathan down off the top stair and opened the door and pulled Nathan back up again and pushed him into the attic and slammed the door shut behind him.

He stood with his back to the door. He didn't try to open it. He knew there was no point. This was where he was meant to be. A glimmer of faint grey light showed through the window in the roof. The rest was darkness. He reached up with his hand along the wall until his fingers found the light switch and then he pressed it. The attic and all its contents were lit for a brilliant moment and then the bulb flashed and popped and he was in darkness again.

After a short time his eyes grew used to the darkness and he could make out the shapes of the stacked boxes and the furniture in the gloom but he couldn't see the far wall nor the wardrobe that stood there. So he took a step forward along the aisle between the boxes and the furniture, and then another, and went forward slowly step by step until he could see the outline of the wardrobe and then he stopped.

He looked at the wardrobe. There was something different about its shape, something bulky and uneven about the door, he couldn't work out what it was, and he strained his eyes, trying to see and make sense of it. It looked as if someone had put something in front of the wardrobe, a pile of boxes, or some chairs stacked on top of each other, dragged them there and pushed them right up against the door.

Maybe that's why his grandad had been in the attic. Maybe that's what he'd been doing in there, putting those chairs or boxes in front of the wardrobe door. And Nathan could only think of one reason why he'd done that.

To stop something getting out.

He moved forward a few more steps so that he could see more easily what it was that had been pushed in front of the door.

Then he stopped again and his stomach lurched and his heart thumped. It wasn't boxes or chairs in front of the wardrobe. It was a figure.

A thin, ragged figure, wrapped in a long tattered coat, and a belt tied around the coat and pulled in tight so that he could see how thin the figure was, and its arms hanging loose at its sides and some kind of hat or cap on its head and its head lowered, hiding its face. But it wasn't going to hide its face for long, because now it was raising its head and it was starting to move away from the wardrobe, coming towards him, and there was a shuffle and scrape of boots over the wooden floor, and the dry rustle and swish of old clothes stiff with dirt, and the soft hiss of whispered laughter.

It was coming to get him, his bad dream, his deep night fears, here it was coming closer, and there was no running from it, no turning now, all he could do was stand and wait and let it come, out of the darkness and the shadows and the black mist and the dark water, cold fingers reaching out to grab and take hold, I'm here, I'm waiting, coming to get you.

It stood in front of him.

His hand was closed around the disc in his jeans pocket.

It breathed in, and out. Stink of stagnant water, rotting weeds.

He was looking at its worn-out boots, the frayed trouser bottoms, the stained and torn overcoat. He drew the disc out of his pocket.

It will come in a form that's known to you.

It spoke. A hoarse, dry whisper.

'Here I am.'

He looked at its face under the frayed cap.

It grinned.

It was his father's face.

Twenty

Vatharos

She lies on her stomach at the top of the bank looking over the edge down the steep slope into the water. The quiver of arrows is strapped across her back. The knife is in her belt. Her bow is beside her on the ground. She has her weapons ready and she is watching the water. She sees the water and she sees through the water. With her spirit eyes she pierces the weedy murk of the pool and gazes clear through to the bottom. That is where the creature lies and she can see it moving down there, its long body undulating, twisting and writhing, gathering itself into sure and solid form. Fitting itself to the name it has been given, to those figured shapes scratched by her ancestors on rock-face and cliffside and on the walls of deep caves. She closes her eyes and can still see it. It is all she can see now. And it knows she is there. It watches and waits for her as she watches and waits for it. Her body stiffens. Her blood runs quick. She reaches out and rests a hand on her bow.

200

He was looking at his father dressed in the ragged clothes of a tramp in the attic. He knew it couldn't be his father and it wasn't his father, but it was his father's face looking at him and smiling and his father's voice speaking to him.

'You found me at last,' it was saying. 'All this time you thought I'd gone away and left you. But I hadn't. I was here. Just waiting for you to come and find me again.'

His father's voice. His father's face. His dad.

It will come in a form that's known to you.

It was still speaking.

'You know I'd never leave you. I'd never do that. Not my lad. I wouldn't leave my lad. And I didn't. I didn't leave you. They took me away. Yes, that's what they did. They bundled me up and took me away and shoved me in here, and hoped you'd forget all about me. But you didn't, did you? You never forgot your dad. And now you've found me and here I am and here we are, together again.'

He was listening to his dad talking to him. He was looking at his dad's face under the frayed and battered cap. This was his dad, dressed in these scarecrow ragged clothes, here with him in the attic, it had been his dad all the time making those noises and calling to him to come and find him.

And he had found him, and he was here in the attic with his dad.

It feeds on your fear and anger and pain. You must resist it. If you don't it will destroy you.

He closed his fingers tighter over the disc while the thing that was his dad kept talking to him.

'We had some good times together, didn't we? Lots of fun. And we'll have lots of good times again. Just as soon as you let me out. Then we'll be off, nobody to stop us, no rules and no orders, no do this and don't do that. We'll do what we like, go where we like, over the hills and far away.'

His dad raised his arm and held his hand out towards him. He was smiling.

'All you have to do,' he said, 'is let me out.'

Nathan relaxed his grip on the disc.

And her hand grips the bow. Her whole body stiffens. At the bottom of the pool the beast is stirring. Its huge wings unfolding and breaking free, its long neck lifting from root and mud-bed. Its blood hot. A fire in its belly. Its eyes bright with the light of its flame. And in those eyes her image is fixed. And in that fire her image burns. As the world soon will burn when it soars and flies free. All this comes to her in an instant and in an instant she's up on one knee, and her bow is raised, and an

202

arrow is fitted, as the Creature, *the terastos*, the shadow-bringer, rises in fury towards the surface.

His father was looking at him and smiling and his hand was stretched out towards him, waiting for him to take it.

'Just let me out, that's all. Get me out of here. Then everything will be all right again. Like before. Only better.'

He wanted to take his hand, to feel his father's fingers close about his, warm and strong. Then the two of them together would go out of the door and leave the attic, and go off and have fun together, and everything would be like it used to be.

'That's right,' said his father. 'Just the two of us. We don't need anybody else. Not your aunt nor your uncle, nor your grandad. And not that horrible Kevin. We'll make him pay, for a start. We'll get our own back on him.'

That was good. Get his own back on Kevin. He liked the sound of that.

His father carried on speaking and his hand was still held out towards him.

'And then the rest of them, for taking me away from you, for locking me up in here. You know I didn't leave you. They made me go. She made me go. Your mother. It was her idea to get rid of me.

203

She got rid of me, and now she wants to get rid of you.'

Nathan felt something like a blow to his stomach.

'She went away and left you, didn't she?' his father said. 'She left you here to get lonely and scared and she didn't care. She doesn't care about you and she doesn't care about me. Gone off to have fun on her own. Well, now we'll have some fun. Fun and games, larks and sparks. And we'll get our own back on her, too. Yes, we will, we'll make her pay.'

The disc was lying loose in Nathan's palm. His fingers opened and he could feel it begin to slip. His father's hand was held out in front of him. All he had to do was take it, take his hand, and then everything would be all right. And that was all he wanted, for everything to be all right.

But was that true about his mother?

He was raising his hand and reaching it out towards his father's. He was going to take his hand. But then in his other hand, in the hand that held the disc, there was a sharp, searing pain, and he gave a cry and the disc slipped from his palm and began to fall. It fell slowly, turning over and over, and there was his father's hand about to grasp his, with its long, thin fingers, its yellow, broken nails. And the disc was still falling and as it fell he caught a glimpse of the face reflected in its surface.

'No!' he shouted. 'No!'

There was pain and there was anger and there was rage and there was loss, and they gave him the words and the voice to speak them.

'I won't let you out. You're not my father. My father's not here. My father's gone and he's not coming back.'

Trapped in the still falling disc, the Creature roared.

Pain and anger and rage and loss.

And she hears it and she feels it and she knows that this is the moment, as its body convulses, spasm after spasm, and it thrashes at the water, trying to climb upwards but it can't take hold, it loses its grip, and the edges of its wings are beginning to crumble, and its neck arches and twists back on itself, tumbling backwards into the opening chasm, and now is her one chance and there will be no other, and she pushes herself up from her knee to her feet, and aims downwards with the bow and looses the arrow, and it flies golden and burning into churning water and she leaps from the bank and follows after.

The face in the disc was crumbling, and the figure that was his father was falling back into darkness.

He watched it fall, legs kicking, arms spread wide. And as it fell it changed, it became a creature of wings and scales and snakelike neck, howling as it fell. And even as it howled it was a crow tumbling in a storm of feathers with a voice that scratched and clawed at the darkness, becoming the darkness into which it was sinking, a twisting ribbon of smoke, without form or shape. Then far off in the darkness he saw a flicker of light, a spark-flash of flame growing stronger and brighter. And in that flame he saw a figure rushing towards him, hair of streaming fire, and bow of fire and an arrow of fire that was loosed in a spray-burst of golden light. Then all was burning and the disc was burning and falling and it fell into the light, and falling too through that light was a speck of darkness, a black ash-fragment dropping out of the world and out of all worlds, into the chasm, the *vatharos*, the lower depths.

Twenty-One

Yiera

She is looking at the sky. It's clear, streaked with red and gold. The sun is rising. A soft wind touches her skin. Her bow and her quiver of arrows lie on the platform beside her. She knows they are there and picks them up as she rises and slings the quiver and the bow across her shoulders and stands on the platform looking out.

The rising sun is before her and all the land beneath is lit and fringed with fire. She feels the same lit fire in herself and raises her arms towards the sun and gives out a long cry, a song of one rising note that flies towards the sun and falls into it. So the people hear her voice and know she has returned.

As she climbs down the tree they gather in the space between the houses and in silence watch and wait, and the Old Woman who has been kneeling at the base of the tree and has not moved from there since Rasha began her journey rises now and stands to greet her. So when at last she reaches down with her foot and it presses on earth, and she reaches down with the other and lets go of the tree and turns, the Old Woman is before her.

'Was the dreaming good?' the Old Woman says.

'It was good dreaming,' says Rasha. 'The beast is fled back to the deep.'

'Good,' says the Old Woman. 'Now you are the Woman and I can die.'

She pulls back a fold of her bear-skin cloak and from her belt takes a knife that is of the same kind as the knife the girl wears at her own belt. Holding the knife in her right hand she reaches out with her left and takes Rasha's left hand by the tips of its fingers and lifts and turns it so that the palm is upwards. Then she gently pulls the girl's arm towards her so that the underarm is stretched out, and places the tip of the knife blade in the soft skin of her underarm just beneath the crease of the elbow joint and pulls the knife point in a line down the arm to the wrist. It splits the skin and a shallow cut opens up in the flesh behind the blade and dark, bright blood wells up out of it. Then the Old Woman lets go of the girl's left hand and takes her right hand and lifts it and once again makes a cut in the underarm from the elbow crease to the wrist. Then she puts the knife back in her belt and lets her cloak drop and turns to face the gathered people and the girl stands beside her facing them.

Rasha feels their eyes upon her. She feels their

stillness and their silence and their waiting. She raises her arms and stretches them above her head with the palms outwards and she feels the blood running down her arms from the cuts made by the Old Woman. At the same time the Old Woman raises her voice and speaks.

'Here is blood shed for the people. Give thanks and praise.'

Then Rasha lowers her arms to the wild acclamation of cries and shouted voices, and to the clamour of bells, and the shrilling of pipes and to the beating of sticks and drums, she steps forward and walks among her people.

Twenty-Two

Two of Us

He sat on one side of the bed and his mother sat on the other side. His grandad lay in the bed with the pillow raised beneath his head so that he could see them. He'd had his operation that morning and he was still a little sleepy from it, and his face was pale and he looked older and smaller, but the nurse had said he was doing well, though he winced when he tried to move, and Nathan's mother leaned over and helped him to sit up a little straighter on the raised pillow.

'Better?' she said.

'Yes,' said his grandad. 'And I'll be even better when I've had a cup of tea.'

'Haven't you had any?' said his mother.

'They brought me one just before you came,' said his grandad. 'But they don't know how to make it in here.' He winked at Nathan. 'There's only one way of making a cup of tea, isn't there?'

'Yes, Grandad,' said Nathan.

'And what's that?' said his mother.

'You ask Nathan,' said his grandad. 'He knows.'

'You've been teaching him, have you?'

'I have.'

'I wonder what else you've been teaching him.'

His mother and his grandad were both smiling.

'How to make bacon sandwiches,' said Nathan.

'Oh, yes,' said his grandad. 'He'll make you a lovely bacon sandwich.'

'He can make me one tomorrow morning for breakfast.'

'I will,' said Nathan.

'He's a good lad, our Nathan,' said his grandad. 'There's not many better.'

'I know,' said his mother.

Visiting time was almost over. Nathan and his mother had arrived just in time for the start. He'd gone with his uncle in the car to pick up his mother from the station and they'd driven straight over to the hospital. His uncle had come in with them but he'd only stayed a short time then gone outside to wait. When they'd finished visiting Grandad his uncle was going to take them back to collect Nathan's clothes and belongings and then he was going to drive them home.

A bell rang.

'Looks like we'll have to be going,' said his mother. 'We'll come and see you again tomorrow, though. Won't we, Nathan?'

'Yes,' said Nathan.

'I'll look forward to it,' said his grandad. Then he turned to Nathan. 'Will you keep an eye on the frogspawn while I'm in here?' he said.

'Yes,' said Nathan. 'I'll go over on Saturday. And after school next week.' He looked at his mother. 'Is that all right?'

'Course it is,' said his mother.

They'd talked about the frogspawn when they'd arrived. It was the first thing his grandad had asked him about.

The bell rang again.

'Right, then,' said his mother.

She stood up and leaned down and kissed his grandad and said see you tomorrow and Nathan said see you tomorrow, Grandad, and then they walked out of the bay and into the ward and joined the other visitors who were saying goodbye and leaving. But then Nathan heard his grandad call his name and they turned and he saw his grandad waving at him to come back.

'Go on,' said his mother. 'But you'll have to hurry. I'll wait for you by the lift.'

He went into the bay to his grandad's bed and his grandad pushed himself up onto his pillow and winced in pain and motioned with his hand for Nathan to lean in closer. Then he spoke to him in a lowered voice.

'Did you go into the attic again?' he said.

'Yes,' said Nathan.

His grandad looked at him.

'There's nothing in there,' said Nathan. 'Just boxes and furniture. And a few mice.'

His grandad nodded and sighed and leaned back on his pillow. Then Nathan said, 'Why did you go in there, Grandad?'

His grandad was staring at his hands resting on the bedsheets. A puzzled look came across his face, then it passed and he looked up at Nathan and smiled.

'I was looking for something or other,' he said. 'But I'm blessed if I can remember what. This memory of mine. It's getting worse. Perhaps I'll ask them to put a new one in for me while I'm here.'

They said goodbye then and Nathan walked out of the bay into the ward. But he was starting to feel hot and a little dizzy and there was a tingling in his fingers. He asked a nurse if there was a toilet he could use and she showed him where it was and he went in and locked the door and leaned against the sink and closed his eyes. His head was starting to spin and he turned on the cold water tap and splashed water over his face and kept his head bowed and his eyes closed and the feeling began to pass. He splashed some more water on his face then turned the tap off and opened his eyes and stood up straight.

There was a mirror on the wall above the sink and he looked in the mirror and there was his face looking back at him. Then for a moment there was another face behind his and something dark flickered in between and across and then there was a flash of bright light that shot through the darkness and then there was just his face again. He stood, looking in the mirror. Then he unlocked the door and went out.

While he and his mother were waiting for the lift to come she asked him what his grandad had wanted and he told her it was something to do with the pond and the frogspawn. Then the lift came and they went inside and he pressed the button and the doors closed and the lift began to take them back up. Then he asked his mother if she'd enjoyed her holiday.

'Yes,' she said. 'I did.'

'It's a shame you had to come back early,' he said.

'I was thinking of coming back anyway,' she said. 'I'd had enough, really. And I missed you.'

'I missed you as well,' Nathan said.

'Well,' said his mother, 'it'll be good to get back home.'

'Yes,' he said. 'It will.'

'Just you and me,' she said. 'The two of us. We don't need anybody else, do we?'

'No,' said Nathan. 'Just the two of us.'

Then the lift stopped and the doors opened and they went out into the bright light of the waiting room and there was his uncle smiling and ready to take them home.

Twenty-Three

The Creature

It slept.

It lay at the bottom of all things.

Without shape, without form, without height, without depth. Growing, shrinking, rising, falling. Ebb and flow, tremble and pulse.

A creature of darkness dwelling in darkness.

Not breathing.

But sleeping, and dreaming.

And waiting.

David Calcutt is a novelist, playwright, and poet. As a boy, he liked reading comics, going to the cinema, and acting out stories he had made up. Among the books that fired his imagination were *Treasure Island*, *Moby Dick*, and *Beowulf*, and these remain favourites. Mythology, folklore, and archaeology are other sources of inspiration.

David has three children and he and his wife live in the Midlands.

Praise for David's first novel, *Crowboy*:

'an immensely assured first novel. It's tense and atmospheric, blending reality and magic and creating an almost mythological feel in a future dystopian setting.'

The Bookbag

'a stunning book, daring, brilliantly written and "staged".'

Waterstone's bookseller